Taming Keys

Charon MC
Book 12

KHLOE WREN

Books by Khloe Wren

Charon MC:
Inking Eagle
Fighting Mac
Chasing Taz
Claiming Tiny
Chasing Scout
Tripping Nitro
Scout's Legacy
Mac's Destiny
Losing Bash
Finding Needles
Forging Blade
Taming Keys

Fire and Snow:
Guardian's Heart
Noble Guardian
Guardian's Shadow
Fierce Guardian
Necessary Alpha
Protective Instincts

Other Titles:
Fireworks
Scarred Perfection
Scandals: Zeck
Mirror Image Seduction
FireStarter
Deception
Mine To Bear

ISBN: 978-0-6451747-1-7
Copyright © Khloe Wren 2021

Cover Credits:
Model: Devin Byrd
Photographer: Furious Fotog
Digital Artist: Khloe Wren
Editing Credits:
Editor: Carolyn Depew of Write Right

Acknowledgements

As always, my wonderful husband and kids get the first round of thanks. They always support me and help me get my stories written. I'm extremely blessed to have such a wonderful family. Especially at times like recently when I'm struggling with chronic pain and trying to still make deadlines.

To my editor, Carolyn, thank you for the continuous support and assistance with so much more than just editing. Miranda for your proofing and moral support.

A huge thanks to Stacey and Kimberly for all your help in regards to Military and Bahrain. Kimberly, I really felt your mother was in our conversations. I miss her so much and have named Donna's housemate Liz in her honor.

Another massive thanks goes to my crew of medical people who helped out with this one: Clare, Codie, Susan and Geri. I wouldn't have been able to get this one right without all your help.

My PA Andrea Rhoads, thank you for once more doing what you do! Fiona and Janine, growing trees together got this thing done. Thank you for the support. And of course, my street team, thank you ladies for all your words of encouragement.

Lastly, to you my reader. Thank you for showing me and the Charon MC all the love you have over the years.

xo

Khloe Wren

Biography

Khloe Wren lives in rural South Australia with her husband, two daughters and an ever changing list of animals!

She started writing in 2013 and has published over 30 books since then in the romantic suspense genre. She writes both paranormal and contemporary stories, including her best selling series Charon MC.

Khloe enjoys writing outside of the box and she loves her heroes strong, and her heroines even stronger.

Charon:

Char·on \ˈsher-ən, ˈker-ən, -än\

In Greek mythology, the Charon is the ferryman who takes the dead across either the river Styx or Acheron, depending on whether the soul's destination is the Elysian Fields or Hades.

PART ONE

Chapter 1

Evening, Thursday 6 May 1993
Bar at Al Layali, Bu Quwah, Bahrain
Keys

"You seriously not gonna hook up tonight? Just look at all these pretty ladies."

With a shake of my head, I lowered my beer before I answered Ace, my libo buddy for tonight. It was just over three months since we'd left US soil, which meant we were more than ready to take a night off. Ace had insisted we come out to celebrate with the locals. And by locals, Ace meant all the visiting Gulf Air stewardesses.

"I got my woman waiting at home for me, man. I ain't gonna fuck that up for a bit of high-flying pussy."

Donna was my whole world. She was back in Texas finishing off her nursing degree. I hated that she had to be in Galveston to do it, way too close to those Iron Hammer MC fuckers for my liking. But my buddy Scout was keeping an eye on her when he could. Before he'd left the USMC in 2001, Scout had always been my libo buddy. We were both members of the Charon MC and were as close as blood brothers.

Ace was a good man, and I liked him. We'd gotten to know each other well these past months, working together in our battalion's coms office aboard the ship. He wasn't as fast as I was with the equipment—I wasn't called Keys for nothing—but he wasn't far off. In a couple of years, I was sure he'd be as good as I was with all the tech we had to work with. And in time we'd form a similar bond to the one I had with Scout. I might even be able to convince him to move from Spokane, Washington down to the warmer weather in Texas to join the Charons with me one day.

Ace nodded as he lifted his own glass to take a drink.

"Must be nice having someone solid waitin'."

I winced at his words. Ace's fiancé had sent him a Dear John letter last year. Cruel bitch had run off with another man and was heartless enough to tell him all about how the other guy was so much better than Ace. Bitch was lucky to be alive after pulling that shit. You didn't do that to your man, ever, but especially not when he was off getting his ass shot at in order to keep America safe and didn't need to be distracted.

"You'll find your match one day."

He downed the rest of his drink before visibly shaking off our conversation.

"But until then, I have all these pretty ladies to distract myself with." He gave me a sly smirk. "I'll just have to run through twice as many to make up for you not doing your part to hold up the Marines' reputation."

"Oorah!"

He repeated the word back to me before he returned to scoping out the women in the bar. I followed his gaze, taking in both the beautiful women eyeing us, and the locals who were glaring. Bahrain was a remote island where the men seriously outnumbered the women among the local population. That made the thousands of air stewardesses that came through here every year very popular indeed. And the locals never liked it when those of us from the US military came in and stole their attention. Attention they seemed to think should belong to them alone.

This wasn't my first time here, and I doubted it would be my last. Thanks to having Donna waiting back home, I'd never attempted to hook up with any of the females here, so I'd never personally had a problem with the local men. But I'd seen plenty of others get into fights for catching the eye of a woman that a local had set his sights on.

A pretty blonde came over and placed a fresh drink down in front of each of us.

"Well, hello, sailors."

I was sure Ace's pained expression matched my own.

"We're Marines, ma'am. Not sailors."

She giggled, clearly well on her way to being drunk. "Well, that's even better. My very own pair of Marines. So, boys, how long are you in port?"

I clapped Ace on the shoulder. "I'll leave you to keep each other company while I go to the can."

Ace knew not to move from where he was while I was gone. The whole point of having a libo buddy was to watch each other's backs while we were away from the ship. But thankfully it didn't mean we had to go hold each other's hands while we took a piss, which is what I needed to do right now.

Added bonus was I'd miss out on having to listen to Ace's bullshit as he sweet-talked his way into that chick's panties.

After doing my thing, I pushed out the door and nearly ran over the girl Ace had been talking to.

"Whoa, sugar."

I caught her shoulders before she could fall backwards. Glancing at her face, I frowned at the mess of mascara streaking down her cheeks as she trembled with her sobs. Even before she started speaking, panic hit me, and I looked over to where I'd left Ace. My breath caught when I saw he wasn't there.

"You have to help him! Oh my God... They just. I couldn't. He's—"

When running my gaze over the rest of the bar showed no sign of him, my blood turned to ice, and had me shifting my full focus onto the panicked woman. I tightened my grip on her, giving her shoulders a squeeze until she stopped babbling.

"Tell me what happened to Ace, in as few words as you can. Where is he?"

She shuddered as she inhaled. "I don't know where he is. They took him. A bunch of locals. I'm so sorry. I didn't mean—"

I shook my head, cutting her off. "Ain't your fault, sugar. You did the right thing coming to me. You good to get a ride back to wherever you're stayin'?"

She nodded. "Yeah, I'll be fine. Just go find Ace. Those men who took him looked real nasty. They swarmed around us, shoved me back, and before I knew what was going on, they were all out the door with your friend."

A sense of urgency hit me, overriding my initial panic, but I couldn't just abandon this woman, either.

"Sugar, do yourself a favor and get outta here in case they decide to come back for you."

Another two women joined her.

"We've got her and we're leaving now."

When they headed for the door, I made my way through the packed room, grabbing Bear and Ghost, two other Marines from our crew on my way to the bar.

"What's going on?"

"Ace's been snatched."

Without another word, they both followed me. When we got the bar, one of the bartenders tossed his towel down then flipped the hatch up, coming through to the public side, his gaze locked onto us.

"I saw the men who took your friend. I have a van. Come with me and I will help you find him."

We all followed him out to his vehicle, an old beat-up van, and as much as I appreciated the help, I had to ask. He'd be a moron to try to take us all on, especially while we were all on such high alert. It would be three Marines against one civilian. But he wouldn't be the first idiot to try it, if he did go there.

"Why are you helping us?"

He turned and held my gaze, anger sparking in his eyes. "It is unnecessary. These men will ruin my business doing these things. Women are not possessions. They do not come here to be claimed like lost property. They come to have fun. Now, we must hurry before we are too late."

Confident he was on our side, I climbed into his van, with Bear and Ghost following my lead.

Keys
Our new friend drove us into the desert at a speed I had to appreciate. He wasn't screwing around getting us to where he thought Ace was.

"What do these guys normally do to the men they grab?"

He sighed at Bear's question. "That depends. Sometimes they just rough them up and leave them out here to find their own way home. But your friend is US military, I fear they will let their egos rule them. Your friend is going to need medical attention. I will stay in the van and wait for you, then take you back."

I reached forward to give his shoulder a squeeze. "Thank you. We appreciate all you're doing for us." Then I turned to Bear and Ghost. We'd all sat in the back of the van, rather than splitting up to have one of us in the front. "We need to not kill these guys if we can help it. I don't want any of us getting stuck in prison over here."

They both nodded, then Bear spoke again. "We need to keep our new friend out of the mix too, if we're leaving them alive. It ain't right to risk these bastards gunning for him because he helped us."

I nodded in agreement. "He's staying in the vehicle. And as much as we're not killing anyone, we ain't letting them walk away, either. I want every one of them unconscious before we leave."

I leaned forward to speak with the driver again.

"When you think we're getting close, turn off your lights if you can. We don't want them to know we're coming."

"They will know we are coming. Noise travels out here."

I looked around. He was right. The desert was basically flat here, with the occasional clump of trees or bushes.

"Okay, well get us there as fast as you can then. Hopefully they'll think we're locals coming to join their fun."

"That is also my hope."

"You might want to get rid of the van afterwards. I'd hate for these fuckers to come after you once we're gone."

He gave me a grim nod.

A few minutes later he stopped behind another parked vehicle. The battered old truck had its headlights on, and they illuminated Ace's broken body curled up on the ground. His attackers had stopped their assault on him to look toward us. The sight of Ace had fury clouding my vision red. I wanted to snap the necks of each one of those fuckers. I was grateful to Bear for the reminder to not kill them as the three of us rushed from the van. The moment they saw we weren't locals they abandoned Ace and came at us.

I grinned as I took out the first one who reached me with a single punch to the face.

"Bring it on, you fucking bastards. Let's see how you do now you're not outnumbering your target six to one."

My words did the trick of enraging them, making them attack with more enthusiasm than skill. The five remaining should have realized they didn't stand a chance against three pissed-off Marines. Using nothing but our fists and boots, we made short work of taking them down, not wanting to waste time in getting Ace to medical aid. I had no idea if any of the men we'd taken out would survive till morning, but that wasn't our problem. So long as we could go back to base to report they'd all had heartbeats when we'd left them, we were good as far as I was concerned. While Bear and Ghost checked they were all down and staying that way, I went over to kneel beside Ace.

"Fuck... I am so fucking sorry, Ace. Hold on brother. I've got you."

His body trembled and he groaned as I gathered him up in my arms before striding back to the van. I wasn't sure if he was conscious or not as I moved, but I hoped he wasn't. That he wasn't feeling the pain from his injuries. Ideally, he shouldn't be moved until a medic could come and stabilize him, but I wasn't sure they even had ambulances here, and I was positive Ace didn't have enough time left to wait for them if they did. To complicate things, if one of his attackers came to before the medics arrived, I doubted I'd be able to hold back from killing them a second time.

I gave Ghost a nod of approval as he popped the hood of their truck. I knew he'd make it so they wouldn't be driving it back into town anytime soon. Bear opened the door of the van and I climbed in with Ace's broken body still cradled against me. Once Ghost joined me and Bear, our new friend reversed, turned and headed back toward town.

"Take us straight to the ER. His injuries are more than the base is equipped to handle."

He nodded at my words but stayed silent. I wasn't sure if he was upset over what was done to Ace or the brutality of the beatdown we'd delivered in his defense. Not that I cared either way. So long as he got us to the hospital in time to save Ace, I was good.

The rest of the drive was made in silence, but I didn't care. I wasn't interested in conversation while I kept my attention on my injured friend. They'd beaten the hell out of him. Considering they hadn't tried to attack us with weapons, I assumed they hadn't used them on Ace either, but I still ran my gaze over every inch I could, searching for stab wounds or bullet holes. I was only mildly relieved to see none. They hadn't needed weapons to do some serious damage. His right leg was clearly broken in multiple places, his right arm looked like it was injured in a similar manner. He'd been on his left side when we'd arrived, the ground protecting that side of his body, so it didn't appear as wounded, but was by no means uninjured.

His knuckles were bloody in a way that showed he'd gotten in some shots before they overwhelmed him. I breathed through the tightness that had formed in my chest. I'd failed him. I shouldn't have left him alone in that bar. Should have made sure he was standing with Bear and Ghost, or some of the other men from our crew, before I'd walked away.

This situation had been avoidable. But I'd failed. I could have prevented the attack. I should have seen it coming. We all knew what that bar was like and Ace had been chatting to that pretty stewardess, who would have turned more than a few of the locals' heads.

Ghost's voice pulled me out of my spinning thoughts for a moment.

"I can see the thoughts running circles in your head, Keys. This isn't your fault. We all gotta go take a piss at some point. Lay the blame for this where it belongs. At the feet of those fuckers who attacked him."

I nodded but didn't say a word. Deep in my soul, I knew Ghost was right, but my mind was refusing to hear it at the moment.

Monday 10 May 1993
Bahrain Specialists Hospital
Keys

We were pulling out tomorrow morning and I was torn. Part of me couldn't fucking wait. If I never saw Bahrain again, it would be a blessing. The rest of me didn't want to go. Not while Ace was unable to leave. But I couldn't stay with him. I knew better than to even put the request in. Ace would be stuck here for at least a few more days before the Medevac would come in and transport him to the Lundstruhl Base in Germany. They'd do what they could for him there before he'd be shipped back to Walter Reed Military Hospital. From there, he'd end up back at his place in Spokane, where he'd be alone. Through the entire process he'd be fucking alone, and it gutted me but there wasn't a damn fucking thing I could do to change it.

At least I could take a small comfort in the fact he would soon be receiving the best care possible. The doctors here were doing all they could, but they weren't as well-equipped as they were in Germany. I'd heard them talking earlier, saying how they doubted even the surgeons at Lundstruhl would be able to save his leg. But I knew they'd do their best to try.

With a sigh, I scrubbed my hand over my face. Even if they managed to save the limb, I was sure Ace's days of active duty were a thing of the past. He was in for a long rehab to fully recover from all the broken bones, and it was highly likely he'd never get full movement back in his right arm or leg. I really hated that he was going to be alone up in Spokane once he was done with hospitals. He had no family left and all his friends were like us—active duty Marines. I'd already decided that as soon as I could after this tour finished, I'd go visit him. See if I couldn't talk him into moving south and joining up with the Charon MC. That'd give him a whole family who would have his back twenty-four seven. Even if he lost the leg and couldn't ride, I'd find a way to get him in the club. Even if he never got voted in as a full patched in brother, he'd still have the club's support.

Standing from my seat, I paced across the waiting room, looking out the window at the desert. I never wanted to see sand again. I didn't think I'd ever see it and not see Ace, with all his blood soaking the ground around him. Unfortunately, until the doctors finished doing their thing, I had to wait out here with nothing but the fucking sand to look at. The only windows the room had faced the desert. I could leave, go for a walk down to look out over the ocean. But that would mean leaving Ace. It was bad enough I couldn't be with him in his room constantly, but I wasn't about to leave the premises. Not until I'd be forced to later tonight, in order to prep for our departure in the morning. I looked down as I clenched my fists, allowing the burn from the cuts over my knuckles stretching to settle my thoughts. I'd helped deliver justice for what was done to Ace. That had to be enough.

Ghost, Bear and I had still been in the ER's waiting area when the six men we'd taught a lesson to had stumbled in to seek help for their injuries. They'd seen us and paled, two backing out of the building, obviously deciding it was safer to tend their wounds elsewhere than risk us finishing the job. We three had stood stoically, giving the remaining men cold stares until they'd been taken back and attended to.

When by day-break, we hadn't had a visit from the local authorities, we'd figured they'd chosen to not report what had happened. Wise decision on their part, since their initial attack on Ace was unprovoked. They wouldn't want the authorities knowing about that part of things.

Unable to look at all that fucking sand any longer, I spun around and jerked back in shock at who was standing there. My body slammed against the window hard enough it rattled in the frame. With a wince, I mentally kicked my own ass because I hadn't been paying attention to my surroundings.

"At ease, Marine."

The gruff voice of my battalion commander had me relaxing as my heart rate began to slow back down. He sat, indicating I should take the chair next to him.

"Come and take a seat."

I couldn't think of a damn thing to say to avoid having to speak with him, so accepting the fact I was probably in for a lecture at the very least, I made my way over to sit beside the older man. He cleared his throat before he spoke again.

"I've read the reports and I've already spoken with Bear and Ghost. I want you to know that if you need to talk about it, my door is always open. Off the record, if you need it. Sadly, this isn't the first time something like this has happened here, however, it's certainly the first time I've heard of that a local has stepped up to help like this. I know Ace was your libo buddy, and that you've no doubt taken on the blame for his attack, but this is not your fault."

I shook my head. "I failed him. I should have—"

I stopped talking when he shook his head. "You're allowed to go take a piss without holding each other's hands, Keys. You did right by Ace. You grabbed Bear and Ghost and you went hunting for your missing brother. There's no doubt in my mind that your actions saved his life. And the fact you didn't kill every one of those bastards who took him was an unexpected blessing. I'm not sure we would have been able to keep you three from being arrested by the local authorities if you had."

I nodded. "We knew that and were careful to not kill anyone. Trust me, I wanted to. Pretty sure all three of us wanted nothing more than to wipe the floor with them. Make sure they'd never be able to pull shit like that ever again."

"From what I was told, it appears the men reported to the authorities they have no memory of how they were injured."

I shrugged a shoulder. "I figured as much, since I hadn't

been arrested yet. We saw them come in the night of the attack. Two of them turned tail and ran when they saw us here. The other four sought medical attention but stayed far from where we were in the ER waiting room."

He growled out his next words. "Fucking cowards."

"Basically. But we already knew that."

He sighed and looked me in the eye. "I'm sorry you can't stay with him and escort him home. I know you want to because it's what I'd want in your shoes. But unfortunately, that's not in my control to permit."

"I know, sir. That's why I didn't ask. I understand how it has to play out."

He stood and clapped me on the shoulder. "I wish I could allow it, but my hands are tied. Know he's in good hands and I'll be making sure he gets the best of care. If you ever need to talk about what happened — or anything else — remember, my door is open."

"Thank you, sir."

I watched as he strode away, my heart feeling a little lighter knowing I had his support. I loved the sense of comradery we had in the Marines, and in the military as a whole.

Chapter 2

Friday 10 December 1993
Houston, Texas
Keys

As soon as I could get away from the docks in San Diego, I'd headed directly to the airport. I'd been torn on who to visit first. Did I fly back to Texas to see my folks and Donna first, or over to Washington state to check on Ace? In the end, I'd decided to head home first and caught the earliest flight I could get on.

I figured I'd spend a day or two with Donna, then head up to see Ace and make sure he was doing okay. I scoffed at myself as I grabbed my bag off the belt at Hobby Airport. That was a joke. Ace was not okay. I'd rung him while I'd been waiting for my flight and he'd sounded off. The fact he'd told me not to bother coming to see him at all had some red flags popping up in my mind. I definitely would be heading up his way real soon.

"Oh, honey!"

When I heard my mother's voice heavy with emotion, I grinned and dropped my bag as I looked around for her.

Tears ran down her face as she broke into a run. Lowering down, I held out my arms and caught her tiny five-foot one frame against me when she threw herself at me. It had been a little over six months since I'd last been home, but it could have been two weeks and Ma would have still done this routine. She was the best mother a man could ask for.

"Hey, Ma. It's good to see you too."

"Oh, my boy. You're home and safe. You're not injured, are you?"

She pulled back and held my wrists out to the sides so she could run her gaze over me, up and down.

"I'm perfectly fine, Ma. I'm home because I have leave, not because I was hurt."

"Leave the boy alone, woman."

My dad gently shifted my mother aside and pulled me in for a back-slapping hug.

"Good to have you home, son."

He had tears in his eyes too, and it was all nearly more than I could take.

"I think we've given everyone here enough of a show, yeah? Can we get outta here?"

With a stoic nod, my dad grabbed my bag before I could and led the way to the door. I nodded at the few people who thanked me for my service as I followed in his wake. As proud as I was to wear my uniform, I couldn't wait to go home and get changed into civvies. Just be an average man again for a while.

A man who was desperate to get to his woman. It'd been

nearly eleven months since I'd spent my last leave with her. Donna had first caught my attention at a Halloween party the club had held two years back. Along with a few of her friends, the girls decided to be brave and come check out what the Charon MC was all about. From the moment I'd first seen her, I'd wanted her for my own and I made sure when the night ended, she was in my bed, beneath me.

My dick jerked at the memory of her in her costume. Sexy as fuck in a skintight black t-shirt and matching jeans. Her hair was pulled back into a ponytail and she'd even found some mirrored aviators. She was my very own Sarah Conner and gave me a whole new appreciation for the Terminator movies. It hadn't taken me long to get her up to my room and beneath me. That had been one helluva night I knew I'd never forget. Then in the morning when I woke to the sight of her sleeping beside me, glowing in the morning sunshine coming through my window, I realized I didn't want to lose what we'd started. That I'd wanted to see where we could go together.

It was the first time I'd ever thought like that. Normally, I was like all the other single brothers in the club. One and done. But from that first night, that first touch, I'd known I wanted more from Donna. Now, nearly fourteen months later, I was actually thinking of not re-enlisting in January so I could have her by my side all the time. She'd finished her nursing degree last May, and was free to work anywhere in the country. Why not in

Bridgewater? Her parents lived there. Surely, she'd want to come back home from Galveston at some point. A shudder of revulsion rolled through me at the thought of her living in Iron Hammers MC territory. They were a club of ruthless bastards and I knew nothing was outside the realm of possibility when it came to them. Every single day she'd been living there, I worried Donna would run across one of them and they'd see her beauty and want it for themselves.

"So, son, what are your plans for your time home? And how long do we have you for this time?"

I shifted my focus back onto my parents and my father's hopeful expression as he waited for my answer. They knew I was up to either re-enlist or separate in January. My father's question was his subtle way of asking me about it. But I couldn't answer them on that because I hadn't made a decision yet.

"Well, after we have dinner, I'm planning on heading down to Donna. I also need to make a trip up to Spokane to check on a buddy who was badly injured on this last tour. At this stage, I'm not sure how long I'll be home, but at least through to the new year."

My mother turned in her seat to face me. "Are you thinking of leaving the Marines, Ben?"

She, and occasionally Donna, were the only people on the planet who called me by my given name. I held her gaze and gave her as much truth as I had to give.

"I've been thinking about it. This last tour... some stuff happened that changed things. I need time to process it all."

Her expression showed her worry for me. "Does this have something to do with your friend up north?"

My heart clenched as I thought about Ace again. Something wasn't right with him, and I didn't mean his physical issues. My phone call to him earlier weighed heavily on me.

"Yeah, it has a lot to do with him."

"Well, whatever you decide, you know your father and I will support your decision. We're both just so proud of you, sweetheart."

I smiled at both my folks. They were the best. Always there for me, no matter my decisions. They hadn't even judged me harshly when I'd told them I was joining the Charon MC.

"Thanks. That means a lot."

Galveston, Texas
Donna

I peeked out the curtain again and Liz, my housemate, laughed, making me blush.

"Babe, you'll hear him coming on that bike of his. Sit down and relax."

I turned to glare at her, but she wasn't watching me. She was completely focused on running a strip of tape over the top of a box. She was moving back to Colorado over the Christmas break. She'd come down to Galveston to do her nursing degree, and we'd become fast friends and soon decided to share a house together, rather than stay on campus. But we'd both graduated this past May, so our lives were moving on.

"I'm gonna miss you."

She stopped and gave me a sad smile. "Me too, babe. But we can always call and write to each other. And visit. It's only a two-and-half-hour flight between Denver and Houston."

I nodded as I blinked away the sting behind my eyes. Thankfully, before she could say anything else that would send me into full-on tears, the rumble of a Harley filled the air and instantly my sadness evaporated.

"And that's my cue to vanish for the evening!" She came over and gave me a hug. "Have fun with your man."

She slipped back into her room and her door clicked shut just as Keys' bike's engine stopped. Pushing all thoughts of Liz aside, I flipped open the lock and pulled the door open as fast as my fumbling fingers would allow. Once outside, I ran toward him. Tears blurred my vision as he stopped and held out his arms. I threw myself against him, certain he wouldn't let either of us fall.

His rough chuckle as he caught me and spun me around had never sounded so good. I sobbed as I buried my face in against his neck and took in his scent—leather and citrus from the cologne he wore. Ever since that Halloween party two years ago, that scent had meant home and safety to me. I'd even gone and bought a bottle so I could sniff it when I was really missing him. I'd fallen for this man within hours of first meeting him. And as proud as I was of him serving as a Marine, I missed him and worried over him every second we were apart.

"Shh, darlin'. I'm here now. I've got you."

With a hand on my ass he lifted me, and I automatically wrapped my legs around his waist, not wanting to let him go for even a moment. From the way his body moved, I knew he was heading back toward the house, but I didn't bother raising my head until after he kicked the door shut and flipped the deadbolt. He paused for a minute, looking around.

"You moving?"

"Not me. Well, not yet. Liz is heading back to Denver in a little over a week."

"Huh."

I wasn't sure whether that was a positive or negative sound but didn't care at the moment. I'd worry about it later. Right now, I wanted to be skin on skin with Keys, so I could run my hands over him to make sure he hadn't been wounded on this last tour. Unwrapping my legs, I planted my feet back on the floor then took his hand. He followed me without comment as I led him to my bedroom where I shut the door then turned to him and started stripping him. The need to see he was unharmed consumed me.

"Whoa!" He gripped my hands and pressed my palms flat against his chest. "Donna, baby, what's going on?"

I shook my head, trying to tug my hands free. "I need to see that you're okay. I need to check."

His worried expression melted into one of calm, of love. "Ah, sweetheart."

He released my hands so he could cup my face between his palms. Lowering his lips to mine, he gave me a gentle kiss that lit me up from head to toe. Damn, but I'd missed him.

"Darlin', I'm fine. No new scars this time for you to inspect."

He kissed me again, longer, deeper and I melted against him, sliding my hands up around his neck to hold him to me as he devoured me. With a groan, he pulled back, and I lifted up on my toes to follow him, wanting more of his kisses. With a rough chuckle, he buried his face in against my neck and wrapped his arms around me, holding me tightly against him. He stayed that way, holding me immobile for long enough I started to get concerned.

"Keys? You sure you're okay?"

He nodded against my throat before lifting his face up to stare down at me.

"I missed you somethin' fierce."

I smiled up at him as a few tears leaked from my eyes. "Missed you too."

He released me and cupped my face again, wiping my tears away with his calloused thumbs.

"You gotta stop crying, babe. Your tears destroy me."

"They're happy tears. I'm not upset. I'm just so… overwhelmed to finally have you back with me, safe and sound."

Chapter 3

Keys

My woman killed me with her sweetness. For as long as I lived, I'd never forget the way she looked earlier, bursting out of her house and bolting across the lawn to me like she couldn't wait another second to be in my arms.

I gently kissed away the last of her tears, all the while murmuring words of love and devotion to her. This woman was it for me. I knew it in my soul that Donna was my ride or die. The only one I'd ever love for the rest of my days.

Lowering my hands, I gripped the bottom of her shirt and started to strip it from her. She wriggled and lifted her arms, trying to hurry me up. As much as I wanted to rush the process to get her naked and under me as fast as I could, I forced myself to slow down. To savor every moment.

"Keeeys."

She groaned out my name, reaching to tug at my shirt, trying to strip me. Then, when that didn't work, she moved to unbutton her jeans. I stilled her hands with a chuckle.

"Slow down, darlin'. I want us both to enjoy every moment of our reunion. I promise, I'll make it worth your while."

Her pupils dilated as she stilled. Yeah, my woman knew full well I'd make it worth it. Unable to resist, I leaned in and took her mouth again, kissing her slow and deep, until she was putty in my hands. As she was sighing in pleasure, I got back to getting her naked. Once I was done, I stepped back and admired her in her bare glory for a few moments before I started stripping myself.

After carefully taking off my Charon MC cut and hanging it on the back of her chair, I made fast work of the rest of my clothing. As much as I'd enjoyed slowly revealing all her sexy curves, now that she was standing naked in front of me, burning me alive with her lust-filled gaze, my patience had evaporated.

Once I was done, I grabbed a condom from my jeans pocket as I started using my words to get her even hotter than she already was.

"Hop up on the bed, darlin'. I have got to get my mouth on you. Haven't had your honey down my throat in way too long. It's past time we correct that, dontcha think?"

Her body shuddered as she stepped over to climb up onto her bed, waving her sexy ass at me before she rolled over to lay on her back. I gripped my cock firmly, and with a stroke, took in the sight she made before I concentrated on getting the damn condom on.

"Spread your legs for me, darlin'. Show me what's mine."

I cleared my throat but knew it wouldn't take the gravel out of my voice. From the first touch at that Halloween party, she'd brought out my inner caveman. With a cheeky smirk, she oh-so-slowly inched her legs apart to reveal her neatly trimmed dark curls, already damp with her arousal.

A groan tore from my lips at how incredibly sexy she was. Part of me wanted to just climb up and slam straight into her, but I wanted to taste her first.

"You are so damn beautiful."

Leaning forward, I rested a knee on the mattress between her legs then dropped down onto my arms, so my mouth hovered just above her pussy. Nuzzling my nose into the junction of where her thigh met her torso, I inhaled. The scent of her apricot body wash was nearly drowned out by her arousal, and it had my heart rate thundering in response. While gazing up at her face, taking in her lust-glazed eyes and parted lips, I lowered and swiped the flat of my tongue up her center, flicking her clit before I groaned as I paused to savor my first taste of her for the night.

"Hmmm. Now that's a taste I've been craving. Brace yourself, darlin', because I'm gonna make a meal out of you before I'm done here."

She moaned as she arched her hips, offering her sweet pussy for me to hurry up and do as I'd promised. With a grin, I lowered back down and thrust my tongue in deep as I used my thumb to tease her stiff, little clit. She cried out and took fistfuls of the bedding as I continued to fuck her with my tongue and torment her nub until she was shaking beneath me, on the edge of coming. Lifting my mouth, I thrust two fingers in deep, stroking until I found her g-spot. The moment I had it, I shifted to suck on her clit, flicking it with the tip of my tongue as I continued to pump my fingers inside her, making sure I got her sweet spot on each thrust.

"Keys!"

With my name echoing around the room, she came, coating my fingers with her sweet cream. Moving my hand away, I gently lapped at her, catching every ounce of honey she gave me, not wanting to miss a drop. Once she settled and was lying limp on the bed, I pressed a soft kiss to her thigh before I moved to crawl up the bed. I made sure my body dragged over hers, so that by the time my face was level with hers and she was caged beneath me, she was squirming with arousal again. I fucking loved how responsive she was.

"I love you, Donna. So fucking much."

Her expression softened, her lips tilting up into a smile as she lifted her palms to cup my face and pull me down to kiss her. I went willingly, dancing my tongue with hers, giving her a taste of herself mixed with me. When we broke apart, we were both panting.

"And I love you, Ben. Forever."

As she finished speaking, I flexed my hips and buried myself inside her deep, hating that I had to wear a fucking condom with her. But maybe if I didn't re-enlist and stayed home, I'd be able to convince her to be my old lady, my wife, and to start a family with me. A shudder ran through me at the thought, and I groaned as the image of her round with my child rocked through me.

Donna

Every single time this man touched me, he rocked my world. No, that's not right. He didn't just rock it, he blew it away. I lifted my hips to meet his with each thrust, trying to urge him to go deeper. I needed more, wanted everything he had to give me. With a growl, he pulled out and before I could say a word in protest, he flipped me over. Then with a firm grip on my hips, pulled me back until I was on my hands and knees. I'd barely been able to take a full breath when he slammed back into me from behind, forcing all the air from my lungs.

"Oh, fuck…"

He seemed to always know just want I needed. This new angle took him deeper and hit all the hidden nerves inside me just right. Within a few thrusts I was vibrating on the edge of another climax, chanting his name as my arms threatened to give out. Just as I would have fallen forward, his hand left my hip and slid up my front, pulling me up until my back was flush against his sweat-slicked chest.

He groaned near my ear. "Fucking love you, babe."

With one hand wrapped around my right breast, kneading the flesh, he slipped his other hand from my hip over to tease my clit. I reached back, gripping his hips tightly on either side as he set about flicking my hard, little nub in time with his quickening thrusts.

"Come for me, Donna. Shatter for your man. Give it all to me."

With a shudder, I did as he asked. My body tightened then blew apart in a massive climax that left me shaking and mindless in the aftermath.

My awareness returned to find myself lying under the blankets with Keys beside me, feathering kisses along my jaw as his fingers stroked from my shoulders down to my hips before returning to stroke again. I lazily slid my hand up his arm until I could wrap it around the back of his neck to bring him close so I could get another of his kisses, which he willingly gave me. I could lie here and kiss this man forever and be happy.

Eventually, he pulled back and with a contented sigh, rested on his side beside me, his head on his hand as he looked down at me with a lazy smile.

"Damn, but I missed you like crazy, darlin'."

I trailed my fingers over his chest, playing in the light dusting of hair there. "Me too. I hate that you have to be gone so much. I worry about you out there. So many are dying or getting injured."

He frowned and it was as though a veil of darkness settled over him at my words.

"We all know the deal with we sign up…"

His voice trailed off and my instincts flared, telling me something had happened.

"I'm sensing a *but*. Clearly, you haven't been injured. Was a friend? Did you lose someone on this last tour?"

His eyes closed tightly as his hand squeezed my hip in a bruising grip. The last of my post-sex glow evaporated as my worry for my man overtook everything else. I reached a hand up to cup his jaw.

"Tell me, love. I'll hold your secrets safe. What happened?"

His lids opened and I stared into the chocolate-brown orbs, sensing the internal battle he waged in regard to telling me whatever it was that had him hurting. I dropped my hand from his face and went back to tracing a finger through the hair on his chest, drawing little patterns there in an attempt to soothe him.

"Seven months ago, we were on shore leave. Ace and I were in this bar." He paused to clear his throat. "I fucked up, Donna. We knew the locals didn't like us foreigners in there, but we went anyway. It was hump day — we were halfway through the tour — and we wanted to get off the ship for a bit, you know?"

I nodded and continued touching him, wanting him to get this all out and hopefully feel better afterward, even though I knew it was going to be bad and probably leave me with nightmares from just hearing about it. It didn't matter. If it took the ghosts I could see haunting his eyes, it would be worth it.

"When we go on shore leave, we always go in at least

pairs. We watch each other's backs while we're away from the ship."

He paused and when I looked up into his eyes, the pain there had my breath catching.

"What happened?"

"I fucked up. I went to the can — the bathroom. You're allowed to do that. Go alone. But dammit, I should have made sure the others from our crew that were in the bar were keeping an eye on Ace while I was gone. I didn't do that and when I came out, he was gone."

Tears pricked my eyes as all sorts of horrors flashed through my imagination.

"Is he—"

I couldn't finish my question, couldn't voice the word but Keys knew what I was asking.

"He's alive. He'd been chatting up a woman and some locals took offense. They'd snatched him and driven him out to the desert. By the time we found him, he was in a bad way. He ended up losing his right leg to just above the knee."

"Is he in California? Did you get to see him before you came here?"

He shook his head. "He's back at his home in Spokane. I called him after we docked, and he didn't sound so good. I needed to see you first so I came here, but I need to check on him soon."

His expression and the way he clung to me showed how torn he was on where he should be at the moment. I swiped the tears from my eyes and smiled gently at him.

"You should go see him. I'll be working most of the time for the next couple weeks anyway, so go visit your friend, then come back to me. I'll take some leave and we can be together round the clock over the Christmas-New Year break, yeah?"

The relief he felt was easy to read as his body relaxed and he nodded. He closed his eyes and blew out a deep breath before he reopened them and looked directly into my eyes.

"You're the best, babe. And if I'm heading out again in the morning, I'd better make the most of tonight to show you just how fucking perfect I think you are."

Pushing me onto my back, he caged me beneath him again and with a happy sigh, I basked in the way my man loved me.

Chapter 4

Keys

It was with a heavy heart I watched Donna drive her car from her driveway to go to work as I started my bike to head up to the airport. I'd found a flight heading to Spokane later this morning, so I needed to get my ass to the airport before I missed the thing.

Riding this early in the morning was cold as fuck, but thankfully since it rarely snowed in the south of Texas, I didn't have to switch out my bike for a cage in the winter months. I'd take the cold on a bike over the heat of a cage any day. There was nothing quite like the feel of the wind against your face and the freedom of all the space riding down an open road.

After getting my ride into long term parking, I checked in and when I got to the gate, I had a few spare minutes, so I unclipped my cell from my belt to call Ace to let him know I was coming. It was nice being back on US soil and having things like my mobile phone. Damn thing didn't work once you left the country.

Ace didn't have a cell, so I called his house phone.

Unease ran down my spine when it rang out, unanswered. Ace didn't have an answering machine, so it just rang as long as I let it. The speakers announced boarding was about to commence for my flight, so I didn't have time to try again. Praying he was just in the shower or something, I boarded the plane.

As soon as I'd been able to after landing at Spokane Airport, I'd switched my phone on and tried to call Ace again. When he still didn't answer, my instincts were screaming that something wasn't right. I headed straight to the car rental desk and took the first thing they offered me. Needing to get to Ace as fast as possible, I didn't even bitch when they gave me the keys to a tiny little hatchback that wasn't much bigger than my Harley.

Once I was out on the road, I followed the directions I'd looked up earlier and quickly found his small house. He lived in a nice area of town. His place was tucked in at the end of a cul-de-sac. Back from the road, the house was nearly hidden from the view of the road with overgrown trees. Trust Ace to work out how to live in a city but make it as though he was in the middle of the country. He'd told me how he'd bought two lots and built near the back in the center, so he could grow shrubbery around him and hide from the world.

I'd been born and raised in Bridgewater, a relatively small town, so I'd understood his need for some space. Didn't understand why he had to try to make it happen in the middle of a fucking city, though. Why not just move to the country and be done with it?

I shook those thoughts free as I parked in the drive and rushed up toward his front door. When I pounded my fist against the wood, it swung open in eerie silence. The lock didn't look like it had been busted in, but that didn't mean there wasn't an intruder inside. Cursing inwardly, I went on alert. I didn't have a weapon, but with all my training in hand-to-hand, I was confident I could take out any threat that might be in the house.

With silent efficiency, I cleared each room. Finding no signs of life, I only had the master bedroom left to search when I paused. I took a minute to just stare at the closed door, dreading what I was going to find when I opened it. I didn't want to go in. Didn't want to see what I knew I'd find within.

Emotion stung my eyes as I reached up and turned the knob. Then froze, unable to push the door in. Like maybe, if I didn't go in, it wouldn't be real. Ace wouldn't be…

With a growl at myself to stop being such a pussy, I shoved the door open and stepped inside. My world tilted on its axis as I took in the room. Like the rest of the house, it was immaculate. Not one thing out of place. Including the man laying completely motionless on the bed. Ace was in full dress blues, the lower half of his right pant leg lay flat against the mattress, making the missing limb a scream in the room. Snapping out of my shock, I stumbled my way over to the side of the bed. I reached for his wrist to check for a pulse, praying I wasn't too late. But the moment I touched his cold skin I knew he'd been gone for some time already. Rigor mortis had set in, freezing my friend in his final position.

All my energy drained out of me, leaving me falling to my knees on the carpet beside Ace. Tears ran down my face, but I ignored them. I'd failed him again. First, I'd not stopped those fuckers from taking him, and now I hadn't been here to help him through the adjustment of knowing he'd never be able to be an active service Marine again. That he'd always be missing two-thirds of his right leg. I should have come straight here, convinced him to move south with me. Got him into the Charons, with a family who'd always have his back. Instead I'd gone to Donna. I'd been selfish and it had cost my friend his fucking life.

I had no idea how long I knelt there, staring at Ace's now peaceful face before I finally managed to snap the fuck out of it and stand up and really take in the rest of the room. The empty orange prescription container on the bedside table explained how he'd done it. So like Ace, to find a way to do it that was neat and didn't make a mess. Would the slip of folded paper beneath the container explain the why? Did I even want to know? Maybe he wanted to rail at me for failing him. Closing my eyes, I shook my head. I was being a fucking fool. From the start, he'd refused to let me take any blame for what had happened to him.

I was the only one who blamed me.

Blowing out a breath, I did what I knew I had to. If I didn't read it, the *what ifs* would do my fucking head in.

I was careful to not touch the bottle as I slid the paper out from beneath it. I knew I had to call the cops in and report what I'd found, and I didn't want anyone thinking for even a second that I was the kind of man who'd force pills down a friend's throat. Best I limit where my fingerprints were.

The note was short and to the point. Classic Ace.

Keys,

Sorry you had to find me like this, but I just couldn't do it.

None of this is your fault.

Forget about me and go marry your woman, have a bunch of kids and live a full life for us both.

Until we meet again.

Oorah

Ace

The tears started up again. "Fuck, Ace. Just fuck…"

What else could I say? I folded the note and set it beside the bottle before I turned and left the room. I couldn't stay there, with his body so close yet his spirit so far away. I didn't stop walking until I was out the front door. Sitting on the bench he had on the porch, I swiped the tears away and pulled my phone out, taking a deep breath as I dialed the police.

The words were like ash in my mouth. Voicing that Ace was dead was like driving another blade through my heart. Making it more real.

Fuck, he was really gone.

Once I finished the call I stared at my phone, wondering who else to call. Ace had no family. He'd been raised in the system. A troublemaker, he'd enlisted when he was told if he didn't straighten his shit out, he'd end up in jail.

Clipping my phone back onto my belt, I scrubbed my face with my palms and waited for the cops to arrive. It was going to be a long day and I needed to get my fucking head together before I had to start answering questions.

Donna

"C'mon, come out with us! One last time before we all go our separate ways."

I shook my head at Liz. "You're not going for another two weeks. Neither are the others."

Basically, my whole group of friends from nursing school were all heading away from Galveston over the Christmas-New Year break. I was still deciding on what I was going to do. I could stay here and keep working at the local hospital, or I could take the position I'd been offered in Bridgewater and move home.

Problem with that was what would I do when I wasn't working? If I moved back home, my folks would want to get into my business and my mother would go back to trying to micro-manage my entire life. Keys would be heading back out on tour in a few weeks, so he wouldn't be there either. I had another week to make my decision and I feared I was going to end up flipping a coin or something to choose, because I just couldn't make a damn decision. Maybe I'd talk to Keys about it once he got back from Spokane. Find out if he was as serious about me as I was about him. Did he see a future for us? He had come straight to me over seeing his friend last night. That had to mean something, right?

"Yeah, but once that man of yours gets back you'll be all about him, so I need to make the most of your time before then. C'mon, go get changed and let's go out. The others are already down there."

"Fine."

With another shake of my head I went to my room to put on something else. I'd known all along that I'd end up going out with her. Liz was right that we only had a limited amount of time left to hang out all together and we needed to make the most of it. Also, Liz could be damn pushy when she wanted something. Even if I'd argued another hour about not wanting to go, she'd have eventually gotten me worn down and agreeing. It was just simpler to agree now and have a full evening out with my friends.

Once I was changed and had added a little makeup and my favorite heels, I was ready to go and headed back out to Liz.

"Who's driving?"

"My car's behind yours, so we'll take mine."

With a nod, I grabbed my handbag and followed her out into the early evening, smiling as I looked forward to a night out with the girls. There were five of us who'd all formed a close bond early on and we'd stuck together throughout college. I was sad that we were all now going our separate ways, but that's how life was. We'd all finished school about six months back and had stayed working at the local hospital together but now the new year was approaching, the others had all decided to move back closer to family. I once more pushed aside the decision I had to make. Tonight was for fun, not stress and worry.

It was about two hours later that things took a turn away from my planned care-free fun. Leaving the girls on the dance floor, I made my way to the bathroom. Once I was finished, I came out of the stall to find a man leaning against the outside door, blocking my only escape. He was a big guy and he wore a leather vest I knew all too well. Keys had called his a cut, and it meant this man was part of an MC, but it wasn't the same one Keys was a part of. Nope, this man was wearing Iron Hammers MC patches, including a name patch declaring he was known as Sledge. I didn't want to know how he'd earned that moniker. Everyone in Galveston knew who the Iron Hammers were, and knew to stay far, far away from all of them. Panic had my mind whirling as I slowly moved over to the sink to wash my hands. What was he doing here? What did he want? I couldn't recall ever seeing him before, so surely I hadn't done anything to garner the club's attention.

After turning off the tap, I looked up into the mirror and gasped. He was now standing right behind me. In moments he had both my wrists gripped tightly in one of his large hands and shoved down against the front edge of the basin. He pressed his body against mine until I was jammed between him and the vanity as his free hand wrapped around the front of my throat.

"You've been a naughty girl, Donna. There's a price for that."

Oh shit, he knew my name. How did he know who I was?

"Wh-what'd I do?"

How could I have done anything to piss this man off? I'd never even seen him before!

"You fucked the enemy. Brought that Charon fucker into *our* territory and let him in you. If you want a biker to fuck you, you don't need to go looking elsewhere. We got plenty of biker dick right here for ya."

He squeezed my neck tight enough I knew he held my life in his hands right now, but not so tight that I couldn't still breathe or speak. For now. Tears leaked from my eyes. I didn't know what to say, what to do, to get myself out of this mess.

"It won't happen again. If you let me go, I promise to never see him again."

His laugh was dark and sent a shiver of terror down my

spine.

"Oh, sugar, you got that right. You won't ever see him again, or you'll pay an even steeper price than the one you're about to. I'm gonna enjoy teaching you a lesson."

He rubbed his hard dick against my ass, and I cursed that I'd worn a skirt tonight. Not that pants would have stopped him. More tears left my eyes as his hand left my throat and moved down inside my shirt and bra to roughly grab my breast while he released his grip on my wrists.

"Hands on either side of the sink and don't fucking move 'em." He caught my gaze in the mirror. "You move those hands, I'll invite my brothers in here to help. And without them guarding the door, I'm sure we'll get some others in here to help with your lesson too. You get me?"

I nodded. My knees were shaking so bad I had no clue how they were going to continue to hold me up. I grabbed either side of the cold porcelain tightly. Closing my eyes, I prayed, begged, this was a nightmare and I'd wake the fuck up.

He lowered his mouth and bit into my shoulder, hard enough I knew he'd broken skin. I opened my eyes and my gaze locked onto the small flecks of red soaking through my shirt from the wound. I couldn't seem to look away.

"I'm just gonna have me a small taste now, then you're gonna call one of your little friends to say you're not feeling well and caught a taxi home. Then I'm gonna take you home where I can really enjoy your lesson. You want a biker inside you? I'm gonna show you exactly what that means."

A piece of my soul curled up and died at his words and I knew by morning I'd be nothing but a shell of who I'd been before this night. This man was going to destroy me because I dared to love a man who wore the Charon MC colors.

Chapter 5

Thursday 16 December 1993
Donna

The last five days had been hell. A living nightmare that never seemed to end. Sledge hadn't been happy with my lesson lasting just the one night. That fucker had come back whenever I was at the house alone. How he knew when that was, I had no idea. I'd looked for strange vehicles or people hanging around the street but hadn't been able to find anything even remotely suspicious.

I was a mess. I hadn't been able to sleep, even if I did manage to get some alone time around a bed. I was working nights this week, so Sledge came around during the day while Liz was working day shift. That gave him all day to teach me my lesson. A shudder ran through me so hard, I stumbled as I walked down the hallway toward the staff room for my break. I'd done as Sledge had demanded, sending Keys a short voicemail, breaking things off then ignoring all of his calls and messages. It had gutted me. I'd give anything to hear his voice, feel his arms around me. But if I gave in to that desire, Sledge would take me out to his clubhouse for all his brothers to have a go at. He'd also threatened Liz and my parents' lives. I was stuck being his little fuck toy and I hated it. Hated myself.

Barely holding myself together, I pushed into the staff room and froze when I saw Liz there. My heart sank because I knew since she wasn't scheduled to work for another two hours that she was here to corner me.

"Sit down, Donna. We need to talk."

I shook my head as I made myself a coffee. A strong one. I wished I could stand to drink it black, but I just couldn't take it without a heap of creamer in it.

"Nothing to say, Liz."

"I know what that fucker is doing to you. It started that night we went out last weekend didn't it? You weren't feeling ill, he threatened you and forced you to make that call, didn't he?"

I nearly dropped my mug of coffee. Hot liquid sloshed over my hand, but I barely felt the sting as Liz's words tripped through my head. Fear for my friend froze me as Liz cursed and rushed toward me. I was like a doll in her hands as she shifted me over to the sink. The shock of the cold water had me waking up a little.

"Liz, you can't let anyone know you know. He'll come after you too. I couldn't bear that—" My voice cut off with a sob, but my eyes stayed dry. I had no more tears to give.

She looked up from my hand and directly into my gaze. "You think I can stand the thought of what he's been doing to you for the past week? I want to gut that pig for daring to touch you. What's he threatening you with?"

"If I have any contact with Keys at all he'll take me to the clubhouse for all his brothers to help him teach me my lessons. He's also threatened my folks. And you."

I went dizzy for a moment as his deep voice echoed around my mind, voicing his threats.

Liz turned off the water and patted my hand dry with some paper towels.

"Thank fuck you use so much creamer. Looks like you just scalded yourself. Go sit down and I'll make you a fresh cup."

Too tired to argue, I went over and sat at the table, resting my head on my folded arms and closing my eyes for a minute while I waited.

The smell of coffee woke me from my impromptu nap. I jerked up and looked at the clock on the wall. I'd slept for half an hour.

"Dammit."

"You're good, babe. Chris cleared you for a longer break. We've all noticed how you've been suffering this past week. Drink your coffee, then let's get an escape plan for you sorted out."

My mind was fuzzy with sleep, so I didn't say a word as I drank my coffee. Once I had some caffeine flowing through my system, I looked back to Liz.

"What can I do? He knows where we live, and somehow, he knows whenever I'm there alone. It's not like I can pack up my car and leave town. He's already warned me against doing that. It seems he likes his new fuck toy."

I heard the sneer in my voice but didn't have the capacity left to care. The hopelessness of the situation had drained all my remaining energy. As I'd predicted that first night, Sledge had destroyed me, leaving an empty shell. A shell I was beginning to wonder if I shouldn't just shatter so I'd fade to nothing. I'd rather be dead than Sledge's long-term fuck toy. He was brutally rough... didn't care about leaving me bruised and injured. And he never bothered with protection. Heaven knows what diseases I was now carrying. I couldn't even contemplate the thought of pregnancy. I refused to believe my body would betray me like that, or to even think of carrying that bastard's child.

Liz tapped her fingers on the table. "You're not working Saturday, are you?"

"Sunday is my last night shift."

"Okay, well, I finish up tomorrow, so I'll make sure I'm glued to your side when you're not working. If you're never alone, he won't come. That also gives us a few days to get your stuff packed up along with mine. When the truck comes Wednesday morning, I'll load your stuff along with mine. I'll just take a little detour via Bridgewater on my way to Denver. That gets your stuff out. Now to work out how to get you and your car out. Would he let you go to visit your folks? If he has eyes on you, he'll see your car is empty of your stuff, and think you're just off for a short trip. Maybe take an overnight bag with you. If he stops you, you can say you're just spending a night at your folks. It is nearly Christmas. He can't think it's suspicious you want to see your folks, right? Especially if you leave earlier than me."

I shrugged. "I have no way of contacting him to tell him. I guess I can only try."

A small flame of hope sparked within me at Liz's idea. I'd been dreading what would happen after she left next week. I'd suspected Sledge would move in once he knew I was living alone. I really didn't want that to happen.

"What about work? If I just leave without giving notice, they're likely to contact Bridgewater Hospital to tell them to not hire me."

Liz gave me a grin. "You're grasping at straws, babe. I had a chat with Jenny earlier, she's worried about you too. I'll explain what's going on and I'm sure she'll be fine with you leaving without giving much notice. We all want you safe and well, Donna."

Sitting up, I lifted my hand to rub a fist over my heart that was now aching. "I don't know what to say. Thank you, Liz. I think, you just saved my life."

Her eyes flared like she knew exactly what I was hinting at before she leaned over and took my hand in hers, giving it a squeeze.

"I won't go until I've made sure you're safely away from him. I can't leave knowing you're in danger. Did you want to call your folks, or would you like me to?"

"He told me he has my cell and the house phone wired. I'm not sure if that's even possible, but I'm not willing to risk it. Could you call them? But not yet. If you call now, they'll come down to get me and then Sledge will bring the whole club in." I paused to swallow past the lump in my throat. "I don't want to think about how that would end."

It wasn't just Sledge overhearing my call I was worried about. After all, I could have rung from a public phone just as easily as Liz was going to, but I wasn't ready to tell my folks about what had been going on. Especially not over the phone. And I didn't want them to rush in to help me only to get gunned down by Sledge and his damn club, which is what he'd threatened to do. Among the other things that he planned to do to me if I tried to escape him.

"Okay, babe. I'll call them in a couple of days. Let them know you'll be driving up late Tuesday and I'll be bringing your stuff Wednesday."

I nodded, struggling to speak over the hope that was flaring within me.

"Thank you."

I wrote out my folks' number for Liz as I spoke, then rose from the table, rinsing out my mug before I headed back to finish out my shift. I walked down the hall with a renewed bounce in my step. Now that we had a plan to get me away from Sledge, I was energized in a way that had nothing to do with the coffee I'd just drank and everything to do with hope.

Saturday 18 December 1993
Keys

With a heavy heart, I disembarked the plane in Houston and went to get my bike out of long-term parking. After packing my stuff into the saddle bags and donning my helmet, I straddled my sled. With a sigh I looked up at the sky, taking in the clear blue expanse above me. Now that Ace was buried deep in the ground, he'd never see the sunlight again. Tears burned my eyes, but I refused to allow them to fall. I'd shed more tears in this past week than was healthy for any man. I was through with that shit. With allowing my emotions to break through to the surface.

An image of Donna's smiling face flashed across my mind and the pain in my chest had me leaning forward over my tank. Fuck. Her rejection still hurt like a bullet to the heart. I had no clue what had happened. When I'd left her to head up north, she'd been her usual, loving self. Then the morning after I'd found Ace's body, I had a voicemail from her on my phone telling me it was over, to never reach out to her again. That was a load of bullshit I hadn't been willing to take without a fight, so I'd tried to call her, leaving messages when she didn't answer. But she'd ignored all my attempts at contact.

With a mental shake of my head, I dropped all the thoughts running through my head and moved to start my bike. Feeling my Harley come to life beneath me had me instantly feeling lighter. The hour-long ride to

Bridgewater was thankfully uneventful. The wind in my face during the trip had helped clear out some of the stress from this past week, but not all of it. Rolling into the clubhouse yard, I lined my bike up with the others As I paused to take in the front of the building, one thought filled my mind—home. This was home.

I loved my parents, but my club brothers were also my family. My folks did their best to understand how losing Ace had affected me, but they didn't get it like my Charon brothers did. The majority of the club were veterans or active service military. They got how hard Ace's death was hitting me, and they'd give me the space — and alcohol — I needed to grieve.

Dismounting my Harley, I made fast work of getting my gear out of my saddle bags and tucking my helmet away. Then I was striding toward the front door, wanting to be inside with my brothers. The prospect on the door gave me a head tilt and opened the door for me.

"Welcome home, Keys."

"Thanks."

Once inside, I stopped and took a deep breath of the air filled with the smells of the MC. It was mainly just a mix of leather, motor oil and coffee. But I'd missed it like hell.

"Brother! Fuck, man, it's good to have you back."

Scout came right up to me, everyone between him and me clearing the way for him. I was sure that one day that man would be our president. He just had that aura about him. He was also another reason I was wondering about not re-enlisting. He'd retired two years ago, and it hadn't been the same since he'd left. Although, since losing Donna, I was starting to think about doing one more stint.

"Hey, Scout, good to see you. Just let me chuck my stuff upstairs and we'll have a drink."

"Fuck that shit. Let me grab a prospect."

I chuckled when he reached out and grabbed a younger man who'd been passing us by and ordered him to take my gear up to my room.

"Third door on the left. Thanks, man."

He ran off to take my gear like he'd been given a reward, not a job.

"Don't miss those days, but he seems keen."

Scout nodded as his gaze followed the younger guy. "Arrow fits in well here, that's for sure. Good, solid kid. He's only got a couple months till we can vote him in. Need to make the most of being able to boss him around." He slapped me on the back before guiding me over to the bar. "Let's get a drink or two in you."

With a nod, I headed over to the bar with him and had the prospect behind it pour us both a drink. Not wanting to air my shit in front of the prospect, I pointed to the bottle.

"Just give me the bottle."

With a grin, he reached under the bar as he spoke. "Let me grab you a fresh one."

He pulled out a full bottle of Jack and handed it over to me.

Smiling, I took it from him. "Thanks, man."

"Welcome home."

With a nod in thanks, I turned and followed Scout to a table in the back corner. Once we were seated and had both taken healthy swallows of the liquor, Scout cleared his throat.

"I'm sorry about what happened with Ace. Such a damn shame."

Ace had joined our unit after Scout had left, so they hadn't known each other.

We both lifted our drinks in a silent salute before downing the rest of our first drinks. The whiskey burned the whole way down my throat, and I found comfort in the familiar flare of heat. Grabbing the new bottle, I tore open the seal and cracked the lid, pouring us both another glass. We sat quietly drinking for a few minutes before he spoke up again as he gave us both another refill.

"So, brother, why you here and not with your woman?"

I downed the first half of my third drink in one gulp.

"I got no fucking clue. I went to her when I first got back. Spent most of the night inside her and in the morning, she was like she normally was. Kissing me goodbye, wishing me luck with Ace. Then the next day I woke up to find a voicemail telling me we were done and over. She hasn't answered a single call or message since then."

"You tell her about Ace before that voicemail came through?"

"About his death? Nope, didn't get a chance."

I barely resisted the urge to rub a fist over my heart as I

finished off my drink and reached for the bottle. Scout sipped his drink while I refilled again and took another gulp.

"You go down there today? Try to see her?"

I shook my head and winced when the room spun for a minute. "What would be the point? Not gonna risk going into Hammers territory just to have a door slammed in my face. Fuck."

I scrubbed a hand over my face. How many drinks had I had now? I glanced at the bottle and saw it was nearly empty. Fuck.

Scout chuckled. "Yeah, brother, most of that shit is inside you. Your head is gonna hurt like a bear come morning. Go on up to bed. We'll talk more later about how you're gonna get your woman back."

"She's gone. Ain't no getting her back."

Ready for this night to end, I gripped his shoulder as I stood and tried to take a step. Fuck me, I could barely see straight enough to make it to the stairs, let alone up them.

"Come on, brother. I've got you."

With Scout's help, I made it up to my room and fell on the bed. He tugged off my boots before turning off the light and closing the door, leaving me with my drunken dreams of Donna. Wishing she was still in my arms, where she belonged.

Chapter 6

Monday 20 December 1993
Donna

Leaving work Monday morning for the final time had me filled with a mixed bag of feelings. I was happy to be going home, to be escaping Sledge and his brutality, but I was sad to be leaving the hospital. It was my first job after finishing college and would always hold a special place for me. I was extremely thankful they'd been so good to me about leaving on such short notice. I was grateful that Liz had told Jenny what had been going on, so I didn't have to voice it. Everyone in this town knew you couldn't fight and win against the Iron Hammers MC. When I'd asked Jenny if they'd still give me a recommendation to take to Bridgewater Hospital, she'd assured me they would. She'd continued on to say that Bridgewater was the safest place I could be and she was glad that was where I was heading. The Charon MC and the Iron Hammers MC had never gotten along, everyone knew that. I'd known it before Sledge barged into my life and reaffirmed the fact. I just hadn't realized how far they'd take it.

My chest ached as I thought about Keys. I missed him desperately. I was used to going long periods without seeing him, but this was different. I knew he'd be back in Bridgewater by now, knew how close he was, but I couldn't go to him. Maybe after a couple of weeks of hiding out at my parents' place I'd be able to work up the courage to face him. Would he even want me now? After I'd broken up with him the way I had, and after Sledge had used me like he had.

"'Bout fucking time, bitch."

I nearly tripped over my own feet at hearing Sledge's furious voice. It was daylight, in the open parking lot of the hospital. Surely, he wouldn't rape me here? I looked up to see him leaning against my car, over the driver's door. Blocking my escape again.

"What do you want, Sledge?"

My voice sounded as defeated as I felt, and I hated that he'd hear it and know how much he'd destroyed me. Until I managed to get out of town, Sledge could do whatever the hell he wanted to me and I couldn't do much about it. Fucking MCs.

"You need another lesson, bitch. I don't like being kept waitin'"

I winced and started to fiddle with the strap on my handbag as I tried to come up with something to say that would soothe his temper.

"Get over here."

I looked around to see if there were any witnesses to

what would, no doubt, be a humiliating scene for me. Sledge was wearing his cut, so I knew no one would interfere to help me and risk the wrath of his club. Grateful no one seemed to be watching us, I swallowed past the lump in my throat and stepped forward toward him. As soon as I was within reach, he wrapped his palm around the front of my throat. Before I knew what he'd planned, he reversed our positions, slamming my back against my car as he towered over me.

I wrapped my hands around his forearm, trying to pull his arm down from my neck, but he was so much stronger than me I had no hope of breaking free. I never had. I couldn't hold in the whimper when he lowered his mouth close to my ear.

"You've been keeping that bitch close to try to stay safe from me, but I'm done waitin'. If you don't make yourself available to me in the next twenty-four hours, I'm bringing my brothers so we can do both of you. Maybe she needs a lesson too."

Terror flooded my system at the thought of them coming for Liz like that.

"She'll be gone Wednesday. She's moving back home, to Colorado. I wasn't hiding."

He pulled back to look into my eyes and his grip on my neck loosened enough for me to take a full breath. I made the most of it, sucking in as many deep breaths as I could.

"Is that right?" The devil himself was in the smirk he gave me, and it chilled my blood. "Guess you better free up your schedule from Wednesday on. I'll be watching for her to roll out and the second she's gone, I'll be there for you. Don't you dare try to hide from me. You won't like the consequences."

He reached his free hand up and gripped my breast roughly through my uniform. He tightened his fingers until I whimpered then with a dark chuckle, he released me, stepping away.

"See you in two days, bitch. Be naked."

Frozen, I watched him stride over to his bike and ride out of the parking lot. I had no idea how long I stood there before I shook free of the terror that held me and slipped inside my car. Locking the doors, I leaned my head against the steering wheel and closed my eyes, breathing slow and steady until my heart rate began to return to normal and my hands stopped shaking.

Once I felt calm enough to drive, I made my way home and rushed into the house, locking the door with the deadbolt and chain before leaning against it and closing my eyes.

"Um. Donna?"

I forced my lids open to focus on Liz. She'd obviously been bringing a box out of her room to stack with the others but had set it aside and was coming straight at me.

"What happened? What did he do?"

She pulled me away from the door and into her arms, holding me against her as I shuddered. I didn't cry. I couldn't anymore. The warmth of her gentle hug eased some of the chaos inside me and loosened my tongue.

"He was waiting at my car after work. I *have* to get out

of town before he completely destroys me."

She tightened her hold on me. "We will get you out of Galveston before I leave. I promise."

Keys

"Time to rise and shine, brother."

Scout's rough voice woke me from my dreams of Donna to a throbbing head.

"Fuck off."

He chuckled. "Yeah, I bet your head is pounding like a bitch right now. But you don't have time to wallow in it. You got company downstairs."

That had me sitting up in a rush, which I regretted as my head spun.

"Whoa, slow it down. I do not want to have to clean your puke off my boots. Here, take these."

Without opening my eyes, I held out my hand and Scout dropped two pills into my palm. "They're just Advil."

I nodded, then tossed them both in my mouth, blindly reaching for the bottle of water I'd spotted on my bedside table earlier. After downing the pills and most of the water, I rubbed my eyes before looking over at Scout.

"What time is it?"

"Monday afternoon."

That had me wincing. I'd drank away two days? Fuck.

"And who's here?"

A spark of something in the back of my mind had me

holding my breath. Had she come? Had she heard somehow about Ace and knew I needed her?

"Donna's old man. I've never seen him look this worried. For real, Keys, I don't think Donna kicked you to the curb because she wanted to. Anyone who's seen you two together knows she's your forever and you hers. To cut you off like she did? I don't believe it. Something more is going on and I think that man downstairs knows it too. Get your ass up and showered then come down. Between the three of us, let's see if we can work out what the fuck is going on with your woman."

Before I could respond, he strode out, leaving me to drag my ass out of bed, strip and get in the shower. The hot water helped clear the last of the cobwebs from my mind and I thought over what Scout had said. He was right. Donna cutting me off like she had made no sense. It didn't fit with the type of woman she was. If she did want to break up with me, she'd do it in person. She believed phone calls were a last resort only to be used when face-to-face couldn't be done. My woman was brave and strong, she'd never cop-out like that and send me a voicemail to break up.

Suddenly I was desperate to work out what was going on. And how much trouble she was in. I rushed to dress and get downstairs, where I found Scout and Paul sitting at a table with three mugs of coffee between them. As I approached, they stopped talking and looked up at me.

"Afternoon, Paul. Sorry to keep you waiting."

Scout nudged a mug toward me. "Here, drink this."

"Thanks."

After sitting down, I lifted the hot brew and took a deep breath of the scent before taking a sip. Nothing tasted quite as good as the first mouthful of coffee for the day. Even if the day was already more than half over. After taking a second mouthful, I set the mug down and turned toward Paul.

"So, what brings you here? Have you heard from Donna?"

He held my gaze in silence for a few moments. I stayed still, but damn, that look would have had a lesser man squirming under the scrutiny.

"Did you do something to hurt my daughter? To make her angry for any reason?"

I shook my head. "No, sir. I arrived home last Saturday, and after a quick visit with my folks, I went down to visit with Donna. The next morning when I left, she was her usual self. I've been up in Spokane…" I cleared my throat against the lump that formed. "I was worried about a fellow Marine. Donna encouraged me to go check on him in person, I arrived to find him…" Voicing it still gutted me. Made it all the more real each time. But if I wanted Donna back, I'd need her folks on my side. I had to be open and honest with Paul. "He'd taken his own life before I'd gotten there. Sunday morning, I woke to a voicemail message from Donna telling me we were over and to never contact her again. I hadn't spoken to her the previous night, I'd been busy dealing with the police and everything. I've tried to call her a heap of times but she's refusing to answer. I haven't been back in town long, so haven't heard anything. What do you know? What's going on with my woman?"

He blew out a breath as he shook his head.

"First up, I'm sorry about your friend. Donna's going to be devastated when she hears what you've been going through." He paused to take a drink. "You know her housemate, Liz?"

"Yeah."

I had no idea where he was going with this story, but I couldn't see Liz ever hurting Donna. They were as close as blood sisters.

"She called me earlier."

He shook his head and I swore I caught a sheen of tears in the older man's eyes. Every instinct I had flared to life, making me sit forward in my seat on full alert.

"Tell me what's going on, Paul. Right now."

He looked into my eyes and the pain I saw in his gaze had my breath catching.

"Some man is after her. Stalking her, I guess. I suspect worse, but Liz wouldn't confirm it. She told me she was helping Donna escape, that she needed to leave Galveston and never return before it was too late. Liz is moving back to Denver later this week. She's going to detour her moving truck via our place to deliver Donna's stuff. Hopefully Donna will be home with us by tomorrow night. Assuming she can get out of town, that is. Liz wouldn't say more but I know there was a lot she wasn't willing to tell me. And I don't much like where my imagination is taking me."

I didn't much like what mine was coming up with, either.

Scout's voice was little more than a growl, revealing his own anger.

"Someone connected to the Iron Hammers saw you last weekend with her. It's gotta be someone from that club messing with her. Who forced her to break things off with you."

I nodded at Scout's assessment as guilt once more tore a chunk off my soul. First, I'd failed Ace, now I'd failed Donna. Put the woman I loved in danger because I'd been so desperate to see her that I hadn't stopped to think about keeping her protected.

"I shouldn't have gone to her."

Scout shook his head. "No way is this your fault, Keys. You hadn't seen your woman in what? A year? I would have made the same damn decision you did in your shoes. Push the guilt aside and let's do what we can to make sure Liz's plan works and we get her out safely."

Chapter 7

Keys

Before Paul left, Scout and I pulled in several of the other club brothers to help plan how we were going to make sure my woman got out of Galveston for good. We also made plans to make sure Liz would be covered. We wanted to keep it quiet, to not give away to the Hammers that the Charons were the ones behind things. We didn't want to start an all-out war between the clubs. Not that I wouldn't go to war for Donna, it was just if we did, we knew a lot of innocents would be harmed in the crossfire. The Hammers had never cared about collateral damage. So, we'd spent the rest of Monday then all day today prepping for our plan.

Now that night had fallen, Scout and I were driving down to Galveston in one of the club's cages, without our cuts. Neither of us liked that we had to leave our colors behind or that we had to take a cage, but we needed to be on the down low, which a pair of screaming-loud Harleys were not, and we also needed the storage a truck provided.

"Can't believe we're actually doing this."

I smirked over to Scout. "Hell yeah, we're doing this. They've had it coming for years. Just sucks we can't claim it."

"Yeah, but it's not worth the fallout. We'll just have to console ourselves with the fact it'll drive them fucking nuts trying to figure out who attacked them and why."

My excitement at what we were about to do overtook my worry for Donna for the moment. I couldn't wait to blow the hell out of their chop shop. They had it in a shed that butted up against their clubhouse and we knew they'd be in church now that night had fallen, so no one, except for a prospect or two, would be hanging around in the yard. We could easily knock those fuckers out and get down to business. Blowing up their main source of income would make sure they'd all be busy over the next day or two at the very least. Which gave Donna and Liz time to get the hell out of Dodge.

We parked down the road from the side entrance to their compound and went in on foot to check the area. Not only did we find the gate wide open, but there was only one prospect out with the bikes, and he was not focused on his job. He had a club girl up against a wall and was fucking her hard.

"Too easy."

I agreed with Scout's whispered words. "Right."

We went back and stacking the bags of fertilizer we'd soaked in kerosene onto the hand truck, we quietly slipped back into the Hammers' yard. Their prospect was still completely focused on fucking his whore, so we kept moving, quietly setting up the bags between a couple of bikes and the outside wall of the garage. Ideally, I would have liked to have the bomb inside the shop but opening the doors would have made too much noise, so this would have to do. At the very least, they'd lose a few bikes and a wall. At best, they'd lose their whole compound.

We didn't waste time getting it all set up, before leaving a trail of kerosene to the side entrance we'd come through. Scout took the hand truck back down to the truck. I waited for him to have it started and heading toward me before I lit up that trail. A whoosh of flame took off toward the bomb, but I didn't hang around to watch. Scout had driven up with my door already open, so I dove in as he rolled past and he took off before I had the door shut. We wanted to be as far away as possible before it all went boom.

We were only a street away when we heard it. The ground shook and I grinned so hard my cheeks hurt.

"That's what I'm talking about!"

Scout was grinning as broadly as I was. "Have to say, it feels good to take out even part of that club. Feel for that prospect though."

"Yeah, I hope he really enjoyed that fuck. I'd say it was his last."

We both shook our heads. That bastard wouldn't have lasted five minutes as a prospect with the Charons.

"Fucking Hammers have gotten way too comfortable with their control over this town. Didn't even shut and lock their gates while all their members were in church. They should be fucking grateful we didn't decide to rig the whole damn place to blow."

I nodded in agreement before grabbing my cell from the dash and putting the call through to Paul.

"It's done. None of that club with be caring about Donna for the rest of the night. Get her moving. We'll shadow her until she's safely in your house."

"Will do. Thanks, Keys."

"Any time. I'll always be there to make sure Donna's safe."

Hanging up, I looked out the windshield to see that Scout had pulled up a block down from Donna's place. Two driveways ahead of us, another of the club cages was parked, with another two of our brothers in it. They'd stay here all night and follow Liz out in the morning to make sure she got out of town safely.

Donna

Liz hung up her cell and turned to me. "It's safe, you're good to go."

I had no idea what Liz had cooked up with my dad to make sure I could get out of Galveston safely. She'd refused to tell me and honestly, so long as it meant we both got out of this town in one piece, I didn't care. I rushed over to her and wrapped my arms around her, giving her a tight hug.

"Thank you. So much. You've saved my life today."

I pulled back and looked into her eyes to see her blinking back tears.

"You go on home, and I'll see you tomorrow with all your stuff. Your folks are waiting for you. Make the most of this chance. I have no clue how long it'll hold for."

I winced as I wondered how much she'd needed to share with my dad to get him on board. As I gathered up the few things I was taking with me, I asked her about it so I'd have some idea about what I'd walk into when I got home.

"What did you tell them, exactly?"

"As little as I could. I didn't tell them Sledge's name or even mention the Hammers. Although, I'm pretty sure he figured out the club connection all on his own. I sure as hell didn't tell the man what his daughter had been suffering through! That's your story to tell, honey."

I blew out a breath. "Don't know I'll ever be able to tell anyone everything, Liz."

She pulled me in for another hug. "Give yourself time. Once you feel up to it, go see a counselor to help you get back to normal. And get to a doctor for some tests. Life will move on, and you can't let him steal your future from you."

I nodded, purposely ignoring her final sentences, not wanting to think about what that bastard could have given me or what my future would now hold.

"Okay, well, all that's left to do is to drive out of here! See you tomorrow."

I rushed the words out, not wanting to prolong the goodbye any longer, or the journey back home. I stepped out of the door and froze for a moment as the sounds of sirens filled the night. Lots of sirens. What the hell had happened? I glanced around the street but couldn't see any movement, so figured it wasn't anything too close to here. I rushed to my car, got in and locked the doors before starting the engine. In the ten days since Sledge had first attacked me, my anxiety was through the roof. Even more so since yesterday morning when he bailed me up in broad daylight in public.

Not only had I been sleeping like shit, I'd not been able to eat much either and had dropped enough weight for it to be noticeable already. With a deep, calming breath, I backed out of the driveway and headed toward the highway that would take me home.

If I could just get to Bridgewater, I'd be safe. The Charons would never allow an Iron Hammer to enter the town to snatch me. Even if Keys and I were no more. Emotion clogged my throat as I thought of him. I missed him so much but doubted he'd ever forgive me for the way I'd broken things off. A shiver ran down my spine as I wondered if I'd have to deal with his anger when I got back home. Bridgewater was small enough, it wouldn't take long for him to hear about my return. Would he come looking for a confrontation over the way I'd ended things?

I hoped not. But I'd take it on the chin if he did. It was nothing more than what I deserved.

By the time I made it to the highway out of town, my knuckles were white from gripping the steering wheel so tightly. I hadn't even seen a Harley since I'd left the house, which seemed too good to be true, but I wasn't going to question it. Even with no bikes around, it wasn't until I passed the *Welcome to Bridgewater* sign that I'd been able to take a deep breath and loosen my grip on the wheel. I hadn't stopped at all since leaving my and Liz's place, not until I pulled into my parents' driveway.

An old, beat-up truck rolled past as I got out of my car, and I spun around to see who it was. My heart rate ticked up when I thought I caught sight of Keys in the cab, but that couldn't be right. Keys hated being in a vehicle, or cage, as he called them. With a shake of my head, I told myself I was seeing things in the darkness that weren't there. Then I turned back to the house and rushed up to the front door. It swung open before I got there, both my parents looking worried. Even before I could greet them, Mom pulled me in to wrap me in her arms. Instantly I sagged against her, content to just soak in her warmth and love.

"Oh, baby girl. It's so good to have you back home. I don't know what's been going on, and I'm not going to push you to tell me. But I wanted to let you know that you can talk to me about anything. I'll always be here, no judgement. Your father and I love you very much, and we're so glad you've come home to us. We'll keep you safe from whatever sent you running."

Dad ran a palm over my hair and down my back, just

like he used to when I was a little girl, and I burst into tears. I'd thought I'd run out of them, but being surrounded by the safety of my parents and their love allowed me to relax enough that all the pent up emotions I'd been holding inside wanted out.

"Oh, honey, let it all out. You're safe now. Come and sit on the couch with me. Dad will go make us all a nice hot chocolate."

I let her guide me to sit beside her and when she wrapped her arms around me, I leaned into her, burying my face against her shoulder, and continued to sob. I cried for everything Sledge had forced on me these past ten days. For forcing me to hurt Keys, the man who owned my heart. For the way he'd chipped away at my soul until I was an empty shell. And for the way he used and hurt my body, making me want to bathe in acid each time he was done with me.

I shed tears for it all.

Then I cried in relief that it was over.

I was home now, safely out of his reach. I'd feel better tomorrow once I knew Liz was out of Galveston too. I prayed Sledge didn't work out I'd left for good and go after her in vengeance. Liz had assured me she had her gun loaded and ready, and wouldn't hesitate to use it if he came anywhere near her. But I knew that wouldn't stop him if he really wanted to hurt her. I also knew if Sledge did take Liz, I'd go back in a heartbeat to save her from him.

And that just made a fresh flood of tears flow.

Chapter 8

Friday 24 December 1993
Keys

Bent over my work bench in my parents' shed, I glanced at the door when it creaked open. Seeing it was Scout, I went back to soldering as he came over to me.

"Hey, brother, haven't seen you around in a while."

"Prez send you for proof of life?"

"Something like that. But I would have come anyway. Whatcha doing?"

Setting the soldering iron on its rest, I sat back, stretching out my back for a moment before I responded.

"Just making up a few things to help keep everyone safe."

Scout's gaze ran over my cluttered work bench with a raised eyebrow.

"You gonna low-jack us all or something?"

I gave him a nod. "Something like that. I won't fail again."

That had him jerking his head before he growled at me.

"You listen to me and you listen good, Keys. What

happened to Ace was not your fault. Nor was what happened with Donna. Life happens and shits on the best of us. You did all you could for them both. I'm not going to let you destroy yourself with misplaced guilt, brother."

Anger tore through me and I stood fast enough my stool crashed to the floor.

"How is it not my fucking fault? I left Ace in that bar to go take a piss. I could have easily tapped another of the crew to watch his back while I was gone, but instead I just went on my way. In the end, it cost him his fucking life! And Donna is completely on me. The only reason the Iron Hammers were even focused on her was because I was a dumbass and rushed down to see her while she was in their territory! It's. All. My. Fault."

He reached out and gripped his palms around my shoulders.

"Keys, I'm not gonna touch the Ace situation as I wasn't there and don't know what went on, but with Donna? She's a beautiful woman, and smart. She's a nurse, for fuck's sake. What MC doesn't want medical people in their club? The only way someone would have seen you go to her that night is if they were already watching her. Whoever the fucker was who went after her just used you as an excuse."

His words had bile rising in my throat. Why hadn't I considered that? Scout made valid points. Donna was damn good looking with sweet curves any man would want to wrap his hands around. The thought of her being forced into the Iron Hammers world if I hadn't already claimed her had my gut churning.

"You trying to tell me I saved her?"

He squeezed my shoulders again before dropping his hands away. "Yeah, brother. Whoever came for her, would have anyhow. I'd bet my bike she was already on their radar."

"You don't think they'll come up here after her, do you?"

He gave me a dark grin. "I'd like to see them try."

I shook my head with a chuckle. He was right. If a Hammer was stupid enough to enter Bridgewater, it'd be the last mistake he ever made.

"That's why I need to do this. I have to know where everyone is, know that they're safe."

Scout folded his arms over his chest.

"It's not possible. You can't watch everyone all the time, especially when you head back out."

I stretch my neck out. "Been thinking about that. Thinking maybe it's time I got out."

Scout nodded solemnly. "The club will be glad to have you around more often. I'll certainly sleep better knowing you're not off getting your ass shot at. You speak to Donna about this decision yet?"

Pain exploded in my chest, causing me to skip a breath.

"Haven't seen her."

He nodded again. "Thought so. I'd heard she was hiding out at her folks' place. Looks like you're both avoiding everyone."

I reached down to right my stool so I could get back to

work. "Your point?"

"Keys, brother, it's Christmas Eve. Go to her. Go claim your woman. Tell her about leaving the USMC. Fuck, go get a damn ring and propose to the girl. You're both hurting and it's not necessary."

Before I could respond, he turned and left, leaving me with nothing but my own thoughts for company as I finished off the tracker I was working on.

By the time I had it finished, I'd convinced myself to go to see Donna. I needed to go over there to slip this tracker into her car anyway. If I went inside and saw her, I might get a chance to put one in her handbag too.

If I could convince her to give me another chance while I was there, well, that'd be a nice bonus.

Donna

I'd left the house a total of two times in the last four days. One was to help unload all my shit from Liz's moving truck, and the other had been yesterday. Mom had forced me to go to the doctor. I hadn't confessed all that had been done to me, but she was no fool. She'd figured out I'd been raped, hurt. The doctor had taken so much blood I was surprised I had any left. So many tests. Including a pregnancy test. Goose bumps rose on my arms and I rubbed my palms up and down them to get rid of them. With it being Christmas tomorrow, I'd have to wait even longer for the results. The pregnancy test had come back negative, but the doctor had warned me that this early on, I couldn't be sure I was in the clear on that. He'd strongly suggested I buy a test from a pharmacy next week to make sure. I didn't want to think about it. To even entertain the idea of carrying that bastard's baby.

A gentle tap on my bedroom door had me facing that way from where I sat curled up in my armchair. I'd been staring outside, watching the clouds float by, wishing I could do the same. Just float away.

Mom popped her head around the door. "Honey? You have a visitor."

"I don't want to see anyone, Mom."

She sighed and looked down for a moment before she looked back into my eyes.

"Tough love time, my sweet girl. You cannot stay locked up here in your room for the rest of your life. I won't let that bastard who hurt you steal your future away from you."

My heart ached at her words, so similar to what Liz had said and spoken in her no-nonsense tone that normally had me jumping to do whatever she'd just told me. Before I could say another word, she vanished behind my door and I could hear her speaking low, too quietly for me to hear what she was saying. Then my door swung all the way open and Keys was there, his big, gorgeous body filling the doorway and making me tear up at the sight. He wore blue jeans and a white t-shirt under his club cut. His hair was still super short, in the high and tight Marine tradition, but it looked wet, like maybe he'd showered before coming to see me. He was clean, while I was dirty. Sledge had made me so I'd always be dirty. Spoiled. Keys deserved better than the broken shell I was.

"Baby, please. Don't cry."

He nudged the door shut before he strode across the room toward me. I didn't move, just blinked as more tears ran down my face. Why was he here? Had my folks called him in the hopes he could somehow fix me? Wasn't he mad? I'd hurt him.

He dropped to his knees in front of me and reached a hand out toward me. I didn't mean to flinch, but that's what happened when he tried to cup my face in his palm.

"Fuck, sugar. You scared of me?"

His voice was rough with pain, like the thought of me fearing him tore him in two. I shook my head.

"Never, Ben." I used his real name, pushing aside the biker side of him. "Why are you here? Did Mom call you in? Or did you come to yell at me?"

He drew back in shock. "Why would I yell at you? Donna, you're my fucking world, babe. I'd walk through hell for you. And no one called me. I came on my own."

I looked into his chocolate-brown eyes, trying to see if he was telling me the truth.

"I'm broken now. Dirty. You can't want me. And I hurt you."

I shook my head. I wasn't making sense, but I couldn't seem to come up with anything that did, so I just shut up and watched the emotions flit over his face. Confusion, shock, anger... in the end he looked gutted. Like my words had been a blade that had sliced him deep.

Before I could guess what he was going to do, he rose to his feet and gathered me up in his arms, then sat down in my chair with me on his lap. I tried to hold myself away from him, but his scent, leather and citrus, drew me in. It brought forward all the good memories we'd made together as his warmth melted the ice that had overtaken me these past weeks.

Unable to help myself, I nuzzled my face in against his neck, inhaling against his skin. His arms were like steel bands around me as he clutched me to him.

"Fuck, babe. You scared the hell outta me. I can't lose you. Not ever. You're it for me. My ride or die." He rained kisses down the side of my face until I lifted up and gave him my mouth. The moment our lips met, something inside me eased. I shifted to wrap my arms around his neck as he swiped his tongue over my lips. I opened and allowed him to deepen the kiss. I got lost in him as he continued to kiss me breathless. When he pulled back, breaking the kiss, he moved his hands to cup my face in his palms.

"Donna, I fucking love you, babe. More than life. I promise I'll never leave you unprotected again. Not ever. I'm not going to re-enlist next month. I'm going to be here twenty-four seven, by your side. We'll get a house sorted out and you'll marry me, and we'll have it all. I promise."

I pressed my fingers over his mouth to stop him talking. He was babbling and being so damn sweet.

"I love you too, Ben. I do. But you don't understand, I'm not the woman I was… what happened." I shook my head. "You can't want me anymore. I'm damaged now."

Slowly, with total gentleness, he wrapped his large hand around my wrist and pulled my fingers away from his lips.

"Donna, I fucking hate that you were hurt. That some bastard laid his hands on you. That club is nothing but scum, and they've paid for what they did to you. But nothing could change how I feel about you. Nothing. I'll be here for you as you recover. I'll be your rock. Your home." He licked his lips, suddenly looking nervous. "Unless you were serious about wanting to break up? If you really don't want me anymore, I'll…"

His voice trailed off like he couldn't decide what he'd do if I did, in fact, not want him anymore.

"He made me break up with you. I never wanted to be away from you—"

He cut my words off with another kiss.

"Excellent. So, you'll marry me? Wear my patch, be my old lady? My everything."

I still needed to tell him about the risk of me being pregnant, but I didn't want Sledge to ruin this moment. He'd taken enough from us. He was in my past and I was done looking back. From now on, I was only going to look forward.

"Yeah, Keys. I'll marry you."

PART TWO

Chapter 9

Sunday 2 December 2018
Keys

Watching my old lady, the love of my life, kneel to place the flowers on the grave of our girl—whose death I could have prevented—was enough to bring me to my own knees. Once she finished fussing with the flowers, I dropped down beside her. Wrapping my arm around her shoulders, I pulled her in against me, letting her cry into my shoulder. Pressing a kiss to the top of her head, I focused on the stone marker that would always stand as a reminder of yet another person I'd loved that I'd failed.

As I stared at Emma's final resting place, memories of her as a little girl flashed through my mind. How I'd taught her to ride a bicycle, how I'd stood out of sight, watching her and Donna in the kitchen when Donna had started to teach her how to cook. Her first day of school, when she'd not wanted to leave the safety of her mother and me but once she had braved the unknown, loved school so much she'd not wanted to leave when it was time to come home. My own tears started as I remembered her calling me Daddy and telling me she loved me for the first time in that sweet, little girl voice she'd had.

Where had it all gone so wrong?

Emma may not have been mine by blood, but she was one hundred percent my daughter by love. I'd been the one to rub Donna's sore feet and talk to her belly when she'd been pregnant, and it'd been me in the hospital room holding Donna's hand as she pushed her into the world. I'd been Emma's father, not that piece of shit who'd managed to both create and destroy her. It'd been nearly twenty-five years since Sledge had raped Donna, leaving her pregnant with Em. It'd been two years since he'd ordered her death.

From the very start, we'd been careful to never let anyone know who'd been Em's biological father. Hadn't wanted that fucker to know about her. But he had known, and when Em had hit her rebellious teen years she'd somehow found out about him. Gone to him. And he'd given her the drugs that had tainted the sweet girl Em had been, destroying my daughter from the inside out for years before her death.

Donna and I had tried everything we could think of to help get her clean, but we hadn't realized she'd been traveling to Galveston behind our backs, going to see Sledge, who'd risen to the position of president of the Iron Hammers MC by then. He'd somehow crawled into her head, turned her against us and got her hooked on his fucking drugs. Then he'd used her desperation to know her *real* father and to get her next fix, to convince her to help him by luring Mac's woman, Zara, from the safety of the Charon MC clubhouse so they could take her. Her thanks for following her *daddy's* orders had been a broken neck.

That day had been hell and one I'd never forget.

I barely held back the sob that caught in my throat. The guilt still swamped me. Most days I wasn't sure how I didn't crumble under the weight of it all. I'd not seen what had been right under my damn nose. How had I not noticed she'd been sneaking out of town? I had cameras all over this fucking place. How had I missed that she was going to see Sledge? Not known that I'd needed to lock her ass down in order to save her fucking life.

Donna shifted in my arms, forcing me to loosen my hold on her. Tearing my gaze from the tombstone, I looked into her tear-streaked face as she reached up to cup mine in her palms.

"It wasn't your fault, Ben. I know you blame yourself for everything that happens in this town, but you can't be there for everyone all the time. Em made her choices. She chose him over us. Chose to help him."

Wincing, I tried to look away, but she wouldn't let me, holding me there to face this demon that had been eating at me for the past two years.

"I have this town wired, Donna. How did I not see her leave? Not once was I able to track her movements out of town."

She gave me a sad smile. "She was your daughter, babe. She knew where every single camera was and worked around them."

I closed my eyes tightly against the tears that flowed down my cheeks. Donna was right. Em would have known where I'd put them. She'd been that smart. So much potential. *Wasted.* It was of little comfort that Sledge had paid with his life for what he'd done. Justice had been served, but it didn't bring our girl back.

Nothing would ever bring her back and heal the hole in my and Donna's hearts.

It didn't help that we hadn't been able to have more kids. Another failure to add to my list. I couldn't give my woman the babies she'd so desperately wanted because I'd been born with faulty swimmers. Well, I guess more accurately I was born with a faulty swimmer factory. But the outcome was the same. I hadn't been able to give my woman even one baby who would blend our DNA together to carry forward to the next generation.

On days like today, it really was a struggle to keep going. Without Donna and my club family to keep me grounded, I doubt I would have been able to keep going all these years.

Donna

Looking into the pained face of my man as he silently wept for the loss of our daughter shattered me. Two whole years had gone by since she'd died but the pain was still fresh for us both. Still had the power to knock us to our knees. Since her murder, I'd done the best I could to process and deal with the loss, and most days I was okay. I could wake up and move forward with my life. I'd gone to see a therapist, followed her advice as best I could, but there were two days a year that were almost unbearable. Her birthday and the anniversary of her death.

Watching Keys suffer was another blow. He'd declined to see the therapist. Not only did he refuse to get help, he also denied the fact that he was having trouble dealing with his grief, declaring he was a Marine and didn't need such things. Which naturally was a load of bullshit, but my man could be damn stubborn at times. And that meant he was nearly being crushed under the weight of his guilt. He tried to shoulder all the responsibility for so much that happened around Bridgewater.

I knew it wasn't only Emma's death that tormented him. I was there every night to hear him as he thrashed within the grip of one of his nightmares. He'd call out names. The regular ones were mine, Emma and Ace, but there were other names. Men and women the club had failed to keep safe over the years. My big-hearted Marine took on every defeat as though he single-handedly had failed them. Most of the time we lost people it was because the club got called in too late, like with Sarah. Scout's old lady, Marie's foster sister, had been held by a cult just out of town for decades. We'd had no idea the cult had been there, let alone holding a woman. By the time we'd found out, it had been too late to save her, but her daughter was a different story. Little Ariel had a whole new life now she was free from that place and living with Scout and Marie.

Staying at the cemetery was only making his pain worse, and I couldn't bear it.

"C'mon, babe. Let's go down to the clubhouse for a bit."

Rising to my feet, I took my man's hand in mine and led him over to the car. I would have suggested we take his bike for this errand, but then I couldn't carry the flowers. That sucked because he was always calmer after a ride. After putting my seat belt on I looked over to his strained features.

"Why don't we drop home first so you can grab the Harley? Maybe Scout or some of the others are around and wanting to go for a ride. I can stay at the clubhouse or head over to Marie's."

Marie owned her own cafe, which basically functioned as a secondary clubhouse most days.

"Ah, yeah, I wouldn't mind a ride. Clear my head."

I nodded, hating how distant he sounded, and shot off a text to Marie asking if she knew where Scout was. I didn't want Keys going out to ride alone, not with where his head was currently. He was too close to an edge from which I had no idea how to pull him back.

Thankfully it was only moments before my phone dinged with a reply.

"Scout, Mac, Taz and a few others are at Marie's so if we go straight there, you boys can get on the move quicker. Take the whole afternoon to enjoy the open road."

As we pulled into our driveway, he turned to look at me, running his gaze over me for a few moments.

"You sure? I don't want to leave you alone. Not today."

I leaned over and cupped his jaw in my palm, running my thumb over the stubble he'd not shaved off for a few days. Another sign he wasn't coping with everything he'd taken on.

"I won't be alone. I'll be at Marie's with the other old ladies. You need to vent, to let go of everything you're holding inside. You—"

With a curt nod, he cut me off, turned and got out of the car, ending the conversation before I could dare suggest he needed more help than a ride with his brothers could provide. With a sigh I followed him inside, my heart breaking a little more as I got changed into my riding gear so I could go to Marie's on the back of his bike. I needed the closeness the ride would force him to give me.

I knew it didn't even occur to him that by refusing to even discuss with me the fact he had a problem, he was pushing me further and further away. But that's what was happening, and I had no clue how to get through to him. I didn't want to lose him, it would tear out my heart. But I could see the writing on the wall. I wasn't enough for him anymore.

Maybe I should find a time when Keys was otherwise occupied to have a chat with Scout myself. The president of the Charon MC had also been a Marine and had even served with Keys for a time. And that man had done some truly boneheaded things in regard to his woman over the years. Yet, he'd managed to convince Marie to forgive him and they were happily married now. Maybe he'd have some suggestions on how to get through to Keys.

Once we arrived at Marie's Cafe, I reluctantly released my grip on Keys and dismounted. Unbuckling my helmet, I shook my hair out as I headed toward the front door. Keys had remained silent since I'd made my comment about his needing to vent. I'd pushed him too hard and now he'd shut down. With another sigh, I walked through the front door, assuming he'd follow me in because I just couldn't turn to see him looking so broken and not fall apart myself.

"Ah, fuck, darlin'."

Scout stood and wrapped an arm around my shoulders, pulling me in against his solid chest for a hug. In the security and comfort of his brotherly embrace, I started to fall apart.

"I can't get through to him. He's pushing me further away every day. I know he's hurting but he won't let the guilt go."

"I know. I'll take care of it."

He pressed a kiss to my temple, his beard tickling my nose, before he released me and holding out the chair he'd been sitting in, guided me into it. Marie stood next, deposited her precious baby boy in my arms and declared she'd get me a coffee and a slice of pie. I barely heard the words as I stared into the sweet, innocent face of Joey. At just over three months old he was all adorable smiles and cooing noises.

I remembered when Em had been this small.

This easy to protect.

I couldn't blink fast enough to stop the tears, so I kept my head down in the hope that no one would see them and lost myself in cuddling Joey.

Chapter 10

Keys

Deep in my own head, I'd followed Donna into Marie's Cafe, not really focusing on anything until I passed through the front door and the sounds of my brothers chatting pulled me back to reality. I looked up just in time to see Scout guiding my woman into a seat beside Marie, who'd stood to place her baby boy into Donna's arms.

My attention was drawn away from them and on to Scout as he strode over to stand in front of me. Frowning, he silently held my gaze for a few moments, until I wanted to squirm under the scrutiny. The longer I looked into his blue eyes, the more I felt he could read what was going on inside of me. As though every shred of guilt and shame were laid bare for him to see, and I didn't like it. Not one bit.

Scout was not only the president of the Charon MC but a close friend as well. We'd known each other since our teen years, although we weren't friends until later. He'd been there when we'd rescued Donna from Galveston. He'd been by my side in the aftermath of Em's betrayal and murder, then by Taz's side when he'd put a bullet through Sledge's skull. He knew my and Donna's whole story.

He also knew exactly how many others we'd lost over the years. Hell, he was raising Sarah's daughter. He had that reminder of my failure in front of him every damn day. How could he even look at me? I was Keys, the tech expert. The one everyone joked about having the entire town wired and knew everything that went on. Yet despite all my cameras, I kept failing. Kept losing those under the club's protection.

"Time for a ride, brother. Let's go."

I looked over to check on Donna, who was hunched over Joey, the chestnut waves of her hair hanging forward, hiding her face. I knew that meant she was crying, and my heart cracked wide open. I'd been so caught up in my own fucked-up shit, I hadn't taken care of my woman. That failure hit me like a solid punch to the gut. Of all the people I'd let down in my life, all the times Donna had been hurt weighed on me the heaviest. I started to go to her, but Scout blocked my path, gripping my shoulder to keep me in place.

"Let the women tend to her, Keys. They've got her covered, just like we have your back. The two of you have been going in circles for way too fucking long with this shit. It's past time we help you get it sorted and out of your system. The guilt is eating you alive, and your woman. And it's bullshit. There is no reason for you to be holding on to it. So, turn around and go get on your fucking sled. We're going for a ride."

With a nod, I tore my gaze from my woman and spun on my heel, heading out to the line of bikes, praying that the women could help ease Donna's pain while I went and let my brothers attempt to help ease mine. Maybe if I could find a way to get my head on straight for once, I could be useful to my woman.

Scout gave my shoulder a squeeze, "Follow me. I know where we need to go."

I pulled out behind Scout, barely aware of the rumble of the other bikes that joined us. I wasn't sure if Scout had managed to pre plan something or if they'd all just wanted to escape the women gathering in Marie's, but I didn't care. I needed this to get my head on straight, and that's all I could focus on.

With a deep breath, I pushed all my thoughts aside so I could simply enjoy the wind on my face as we headed west, away from Bridgewater. It was nearly an hour later when my heart rate ticked up a notch as I realized where Scout was taking us. He led us up an old driveway I remembered all too well, and headed toward the large, bare patch of ground where a giant barn had once stood. I rolled to a stop beside him and following his lead, cut my engine but didn't get off my machine. Taz and Mac came up on either side of us, while the others stopped behind us. The four of us just sat there staring at the few charred bits that were all that remained of what had once been there as we remembered.

"That fucker died too easy."

I nodded at Taz's words as Scout responded. "You did what was best in the moment, brother. Clean shot to the head ended his reign of terror and prevented him from hurting Zara any further. Yeah, it would have been fucking nice to take out some of our frustrations on beating the holy hell outta him before he died, but ultimately, what we needed was him dead and gone."

I turned to look at Mac, who was frowning at one of the charred posts, waiting for him to sense my gaze and look at me before I said what I needed to.

"I'm sorry, Mac. I should have known what Em was doing, sneaking down to Galveston. I definitely should have seen Sledge and his lackeys had come into Bridgewater that day."

He held his palm up to silence me. "Keys, stop that shit, brother. In the end, you saved Zara. Without you tracking her phone out here, leading us straight to where she was, she'd have been dead. Or so fucking messed up she'd have wished for death. You have nothing to be sorry for. Sure, Em was your daughter and she went off the rails, betrayed the club — her family—but that was *her* choice. Hell, man, we all made dumb decisions when we were young. Trusted the wrong people. Lucky for us, we all survived the lesson. Sadly, Em wasn't so lucky. Can't tell you how fucking sorry I am that you and Donna had to bury her long before her time. But, Keys, it wasn't your fault. You've let this shit eat you up for years and it's not necessary, or right."

He paused and scrubbed a hand over his face with a sigh

before he looked back at me. "You know that's what guts us all the most, right? The way you and Donna are still fucking hurting so badly over it. We're your fucking family, man. Let us help you here. Tell us what you need from us to get you back level. Because you're gonna burn yourself out soon if you keep up what you're doing. And if you keep pushing your old lady away, she'll either find somewhere else to be or crash and burn right along with you."

I stilled, before shifting my gaze from Mac to Taz, then Scout. "We've all noticed how much time you spend on your computer, watching all your cameras twenty-four/seven. It ain't healthy, brother. If you believe we need to keep an eye on them at all times, you ask for fucking help. Take a couple of brothers, maybe a few of the prospects, and train them up. Hell, we'll start a security company if we have to, and fucking pay them to keep watch. You can't do it on your own, no one person could. Bridgewater's too big."

To hide the swell of emotion making my eyes sting, I shook my head and forced out a laugh. "So how long you been planning this little intervention, Scout?"

I looked back to the charred shit in front of us and let the memories take me back. The weather over the past two years had taken care of a lot of the remains of the fire we'd set, but not all of it. As I stared at the blackened bits of timber, I recalled in vivid detail what we'd found back then.

As soon as I'd traced Zara's location, Scout and Taz had

ridden out with Mac while I'd joined Donna in the tank
— the club's own ambulance. Years ago, we'd kitted out
the vehicle with everything it would need to get in or out
of just about anywhere and be a fully functioning
ambulance. It was my and Donna's baby.

We'd rolled up with the rest of the club that rainy night
to discover a bloodbath inside. Sledge and two other Iron
Hammers were dead, and Mac had been sitting, holding
Zara sideways on his lap, facing away from us. She was
naked and her back had been viciously whipped from her
neck to her ass. Mac had looked like a man ruined as he'd
sat there carefully nursing his woman. As though by
holding her to him, he could hold her to earth.

As we'd loaded her up and got her ready for transport to
the hospital, I'd heard Scout order the others to deal with
the bodies then burn the barn down. I had no clue who'd
had the honor of setting the blaze, not that it mattered. So
long as it got done.

This place had been Sledge's place. He'd bought it,
putting one of the Iron Hammers company names on the
deed. We were on friendly terms with the new crew
running the club now so knew that they hadn't bothered
with even coming to check out the place since the shift
of leadership, so it had sat here untouched. It was about
an hour ride southwest of Bridgewater, a long way from
the boundaries of what the Charon MC considered our
area and as far as I knew, this was the first time anyone
from the club had returned.

Neither Scout nor the others had answered me, not that

they needed to. They were right to call me on my shit. I was running myself and my old lady into the ground, had been for years. It was time to stop blindly digging myself a hole that was rapidly getting too deep to climb out of.

I cleared my throat. "A team sounds good. Setting up a security company would give the general public, the ones too scared to reach out to an MC, somewhere to go to. It'll be easier to protect the town as a whole."

Scout nodded. "We'll bring it up at church tomorrow and get the ball rolling. Sooner we get it set up, the sooner you can take a step back and breathe a little. Maybe take your woman on a fucking vacation or something."

The thought of taking Donna away for a while had me smiling. "Yeah, I'm sure she'd love that. Can't remember the last time we took some time off together."

Scout reached over and gave my shoulder a squeeze. "Exactly, my friend. And that shit ain't right. You and Donna need to take some time away and reconnect, even if it's only for a night. The town will survive that long without its eye in the sky watching."

He was right, and I needed to start looking after my woman and myself…right fucking now. I'd begin making calls now, but there was no service out here.

"Soon as we get back, I'll make the calls. Donna and I will be taking next weekend off."

"Good to hear. Now, let's get the fuck away from this place and ride."

He circled his finger in the air and we all started our sleds up and headed out. I hoped Scout didn't plan on going straight back to Marie's. It had been a damn long time since we'd gone for a nice long ride for no reason other than to feel the wind on our faces. I wasn't ready for it to be over yet.

Donna

After the men had all headed out, Marie set a mug and plate in front of me before she moved to take her seat beside me again. Everyone knew what today was, could guess why I was upset, and I appreciated they let me be while I got my shit back in its box. By the time I'd finished my coffee, eaten my pie and had enough baby cuddles with Joey to soothe my heart, I was feeling more human and ready to join in the conversation going on around me.

The club's newest business, Hera Daycare, was being run by Bess' mother-in-law, Barbara, so Bess was entertaining everyone with stories of opening week. I couldn't help smiling as she told a story that involved the sweet, innocent boy I was holding and Barbara.

Marie was shaking her head, trying to hold in her laughter. "No way. My son would never do such a thing."

I gave Joey's nose a tweak. "I bet he did it on purpose. Didn't you, little man? It wasn't your momma changing your diaper, so you set the sprinkler going, didn't you?"

He gave me a grin and a coo that melted me and had us all laughing.

When Bess got her chuckling under control, she wiped her eyes and cleared her throat. "I shouldn't laugh, but it really was funny. Poor Barbara. Hopefully she'll turn up tomorrow."

Since it was Sunday afternoon, the center was not open today, hence we had Bess here to chat with us and little Joey for cuddles. The cafe used to be closed on Sunday's too, but Marie had started opening it seven days a week a while back, now that she had more employees she could trust to run things. Marie herself wasn't technically working today, but was here to catch up with all of us.

"Where is Barbara? She knows she's welcome to join us, right?"

Bess rolled her eyes. "Ashlynn begged for a Grandma-Granddaughter day and we all know Barbara cannot say no to that girl. It worked out well since Needles is working most of the day down at Silky Ink and I wanted to come hang out here with y'all."

Marie snickered again. "It's even funnier that Ashlynn managed to convince Barbara to take Ariel as well. Those two can weave a story, I tell you. Had us all feeling like hell because poor little Ariel has no grandma of her own."

Bess shook her head. "Those two together are a force of nature. We're going to be in for it when they're teenagers."

Marie shuddered. "I don't want to think about it."

Remembering one of the girls' earlier plans I didn't recall hearing the ending of I spoke up. "What happened about that horse they wanted?"

Bess dropped her head over onto Flick's shoulder with a dramatic groan, making the rest of us laugh.

"Those girls somehow managed to contact someone about a damn horse they had for sale. I got an email with a sales contract and address to mail it with a certified check for purchase. The owners didn't sound very happy they'd been scammed by horse-crazy kids. Heaven forbid those two get hold of our credit card information!"

That had me smiling wistfully at a memory of Emma. "Em brought home a goat once. She'd arranged to buy it off a kid in her class who lived on a farm. She must have been around ten years old."

That set off another round of laughter that I couldn't help but join.

"Seriously? A goat? How the hell did she get it home?"

I gave Flick a smirk. "She walked it on a leash, of course. I can still remember the look of horror on Keys' face when Em came through the door, proud as you please, leading this little goat on a damn dog leash."

Joey started squirming so I shifted him so he could see everyone. When he still wasn't happy, I passed him back to Marie.

"What happened to it?"

"What could we do? We stuck it in the backyard and it mowed our lawn, and trimmed the trees, and ate various pieces of washing for the next two years before Keys finally had enough and found a farmer to take it."

Rose shook her head. "I remember that. Em was mad at Keys for a month after he sold that goat."

"Which was nuts, because after the first few months she lost all interest in the damn animal!"

Rose wagged her finger at me. "Ah, but you're forgetting, teenagers aren't supposed to make sense."

The rumble of Harleys filtering through into the shop stopped the conversation as we all turned to watch our men pull up out the front and dismount their rides.

"Hmm. Never gets old watching our men on their machines."

I nodded at Marie's words since I'd just been thinking the same thing. They all came striding in and I was relieved to see Keys looking happier, more settled than he'd been earlier. He came over and when he held his hand out to me, I took it and allowed him to pull me to my feet and in against him. He wrapped his arms around my waist as I rested my palms on his chest. Rising up onto my toes, I wanted to press a kiss to the corner of his mouth, but he turned his head so our lips met. He took control and deepened the kiss, making my heart swell. Holding me tightly against him, he devoured my mouth in a way he hadn't for a long damn time. Tears pricked my eyes at having my domineering caveman back at last.

"Get a room!"

Laughter echoed around us as we broke apart and heat flashed across my cheeks. Keys grinned at me, looking ten years younger than he had this morning. "How about we take Taz's suggestion and head on home to find that room?"

Biting my lip, I wasn't sure what to say as

embarrassment and arousal mixed within me. Keys just continued to grin down at me before he turned to the others.

"We'll catch you all later. Thanks for the ride, brothers."

With his warm palm against my lower back, he guided me out to his bike.

Chapter 11

Keys

It was with a much lighter heart that I rode home from Marie's with Donna behind me, where she belonged. Her arms wrapped around my waist, her breasts pressed against my back. I couldn't believe how different the world looked now compared to just hours earlier.

A lot of the shit I'd been feeling this morning was still there, weighing me down, but with Scout's idea of a security team to help monitor everything, I could see a way forward. A way to prevent further losses in the future. A way to share the fucking load. Because he'd been right. Bridgewater was too big for just me to monitor everything, and that's what I'd been trying to do. It took so much of my time, I barely saw Donna most days. And it had been a long damn time since I'd been inside my woman, felt her wrapped around me. Showed her how much I fucking loved her.

That was changing tonight.

This morning might have been a clusterfuck. Today might be the second anniversary of burying our daughter, but dammit, we were going to end the day right.

Once I'd parked and we were both off my bike and our helmets stowed, I took her hand and led her up the path to the house. Making fast work of unlocking things, I got us both inside and kicked the door shut. Before she could utter a word, I shoved Donna up against the wood and had my mouth on hers. With a moan, she relaxed against me and opened her lips, darting her tongue out to dance with mine. It didn't take long before I wanted—needed—more. I reached for the bottom of her shirt and lifted it up, breaking the kiss only long enough to lift it off her, before I was back at her. Fuck, I'd missed this. This heat and urgency that had always been between us.

She wrapped her arms around my neck and lifted a leg to wrap around my hip. Taking the hint, I gripped her ass and lifted her, enabling her to wrap both her legs around my waist. Her pussy ground against my hard cock, the layers of denim doing nothing to lessen the impact of feeling her heat against me.

"Fuck, Donna."

With a whimper, she peppered kisses across my cheek until she got to my ear, where she nipped the lobe. My cock throbbed in response and I turned to head to the bedroom. As I passed the kitchen table, I grinned and changed direction. Fuck taking my woman to bed. I'd do that when we were ready for sleep. We might be older than we once were, but we weren't so old I couldn't fuck my woman in any room of the house I damn well wanted to.

Setting her on the edge of the table, I flipped her bra catch open then dropped to my knees to take her boots off, looking up as she peeled the lacy material off her breasts. I stopped and rubbed her feet for a few moments as I absorbed the sight she made. When she moved to cross her arms over herself, I shook my head and reached over to tweak her nipple.

"Don't, babe. Fucking love looking at you and all your sexy curves."

Pink flashed across her cheeks as she smirked at me. "Wouldn't mind takin' in your curves, if only you weren't wearing so much."

With a laugh, I stood and toed off my boots, stripping out of my cut and shirt. "Glad you like the dad bod I've got going on."

Telling me I've got curves? Dammit. I might not be rocking a six pack like I had back in the day, but I was no slouch... as I proved just now by carrying her around the house.

She slipped off the table and resting her palms on my pecs, leaned up to press a kiss to the corner of my mouth, as she liked to do. "I love you, Ben. All of you. Dad bod and all."

Grunting, I tried to fight the urge to laugh at her antics as I went for the fly of her jeans, nearly tearing the damn zipper off in my haste to get to what lay beneath, all the while kissing her sassy fucking mouth. Her hands didn't stay idle but went for my pants and it wasn't long till we were both naked.

Wrapping my palms around either side of her waist, I lifted her up so she was sitting on the edge of the table again. Leaving her mouth, I kissed my way down her body, stopping to suck on each of her nipples until she was squirming and gripping a hand in my hair, trying to hold me in place. But I wasn't done with this exploration. Not by a long shot.

Shifting down, I kissed my way over her softly rounded tummy and down to her pussy. Dropping to my knees, I held her open with my thumbs and licked my tongue up her center, making sure to hit her clit before I pulled back to do it again.

"Ben!"

With a grin I added two fingers to the mix, making sure I hit her g-spot on each thrust I made into her wet heat. When she wrapped her fingers in my hair again, pulling my mouth back to her core, I hummed against her clit, sending her over the edge. I lapped up every drop of cream she gave me before I rose up and thrust my dick deep inside her before she had time to fully recover from her first orgasm. I hitched her leg up so she was spread wider and I could get in deep with each thrust. The whole time I kept my gaze locked on hers, making sure I didn't miss a fucking moment of the way her eyes glazed over when she was this aroused. How a blush would spread across her chest and up her neck when she came for me. Damn, but I'd missed this.

"I love you, Donna. You're my world. You know that, right?"

Donna

I had no damn idea what happened on the ride the men had gone on earlier, but whatever it was, I hoped they planned on doing it on a regular basis in the future. I couldn't remember the last time Keys had been so hot for me that he couldn't wait till we made it to the bedroom. I was probably going to be sore in the morning from acting like I was twenty years younger than I was, but I really, really didn't give a damn. Every ache would be worth it. Keys had been insatiable, not stopping until he'd had me screaming his name twice on the table before he'd carried me in here to our bedroom. Then he'd laid me out and loved on me sweet and gentle. When we'd come together a few minutes ago, I'd started crying with the overwhelming emotions I had swirling within me, which panicked Keys.

"You sure I didn't hurt you?"

I lay snuggled up against him, my head resting on one of his biceps, while he stroked his free hand down my hair and back. I looked up into his face with a sniffle.

"I promise you didn't. You'd never hurt me. It was just very intense. Not all tears are unhappy ones."

He squeezed his eyes shut for a moment before he leaned in to press a kiss to my forehead.

"That ain't true, love. I've been hurting you for months. Years. I didn't mean for it to get so out of hand. I didn't realize it had until Scout and Mac called me on it earlier. It forced me to see what I'd been doing, and what, or rather who, I'd been neglecting."

I rubbed my nose against the hair on his chest, pressing a kiss over his heart before I looked back up at him.

"You did what you could to cope. I know you, Ben. I know how you need to watch over everyone. I might not always like how much time it takes you away from me, but the way you can jump in and provide the information needed to save those we care about is worth it. Like that time you found Ariel when she'd wandered off. Things like that make the sacrifice all worthwhile."

Soon after Scout and Marie had taken Ariel in, she'd snuck out of the house and taken off. Everyone was in a panic until Keys had turned up, laptop in hand, to tell them where she was. Poor little love had gone to the cemetery to visit her mom's grave. He'd been able to save the day because he'd low-jacked Ariel's shoes and a couple of her toys and bags. I was pretty sure he'd done the same thing to everyone in the club that he could—not just the kids—but he was very close-lipped about who, exactly, he had eyes on. He would never, and I mean never, invade someone's privacy without a damn good reason.

"Nothing is worth losing you. We've been drifting and a lot of that is on me. Donna, I promise I'll do better. Spend more time with you, get a better work/life balance."

As he'd spoken, my mind started to churn. He wasn't

the only one who'd buried himself in work. My heart ached at how stupid I'd been, how I'd let things slide as much as Keys had.

"It wasn't just you neglecting us. I did the same. I didn't even realize until just now that I've been doing the same damn thing as you. Burying myself in work instead of trying to spend time with you. I should have been helping you monitor things. I'm your wife, Ben, I should have been by your side, helping you. Instead, I was at the hospital taking care of everyone else except the one who matters the most to me."

Tears filled my eyes as I looked up into Keys' face. "Forgive me?"

"Ah fuck, darlin'. We're a pair, aren't we?" He leaned down to press a soft kiss to my lips. "There's nothing to forgive, babe. How about we go away next weekend? Head up to Fort Worth for a night or two. Have some alone time."

Happiness filled me at the idea. "That would be great. A whole weekend to ourselves. But are you sure? If something happens while we're gone, you'd never forgive yourself."

Neither would I, but the last thing Keys needed was more guilt.

"Scout suggested we get a team together to help me keep up with everything I do. We're starting a new business, a security company. We're going to bring it to church tomorrow and see who's interested. Hopefully I'll get enough volunteers within the club to get it off the ground and running. I don't want strangers I don't personally trust to have the access I do."

I was tracing my fingers through his chest hair again as I thought over what he was saying.

"You should ask Flick. I know you men will huff and puff about it being men's work to protect everyone, but she did work for the FBI. She could be really helpful in getting things set up, and I know she gets bored working at the gun range."

Flick's uncle owned the local range and she helped out over there, along with her husband, Taz, when she wasn't chasing around their little girl.

Keys stiffened and I glanced up at his frowning face to see what had him freaking out.

"How did you know about Flick?"

Ah, that's what he was worried about. Me knowing "club secrets". Honestly, I think the men would be surprised at how much us old ladies really knew. We weren't fools. We could read between the lines, and we also talked to each other. Apparently, a lot more than the men realized. I chuckled. "Oh, honey, women talk. We know all about how she came to town as an undercover agent to try to get Taz back into the fold."

His frown stayed in place. "You shouldn't know that. Who else knows?"

I shifted so I could press a kiss to the corner of his mouth before I pulled back and smoothed away his frown lines with my fingertips.

"Old ladies know how to keep secrets, babe. Stop

worrying. No one knows that'll tell someone they shouldn't."

He grunted but thankfully let the topic drop. I was pretty sure he'd be bringing it up with the other men, though, so I made a mental note to text the other ladies later to warn them. Then Keys' hands began to roam once more, and I stopped thinking about anything other than how much I loved my man.

Mirabelle

Pulling the crisp, white sheet back, I slid in and pulled the covers up high around my throat. It was time for lights out, signaling that another day was over. With a deep breath, I closed my eyes and tried to imagine sheep jumping over a fence. That was supposed to help you go to sleep, right? Although I honestly didn't know why I even tried anymore. It never worked. No matter what I did, I always struggled to get to sleep. And once I did finally manage to nod off, or if I took the sleeping pills they gave me, the terror of my past would haunt my dreams until I woke in a panic.

Pastor Godfrey had been the devil himself. He'd tricked me into thinking he'd been my savior, that he'd loved and cared for me, but the reality was I'd been a naive fool and he'd taken advantage of it. He'd taken possession of all my parents' assets after they died, including me. He'd had some new drug that he'd use on me daily. On that evil stuff I'd turn into a sex-crazed demon, but once it wore off, I'd go back to being my sweet, naive self with no memory of what I'd done.

From what the authorities could piece together, he'd used it nightly on me then had his men *train* me. When they'd started to trace back his movements prior to coming to Bridgewater, they'd discovered that was what he liked to do. He'd move to a new town and take in one or more teens or adults to "rescue." He'd brainwash them into being his little puppets during the day. Just like he'd had me doing, they'd go out and tell the world how wonderful he was. Then, at night, they'd be his sex slaves. When he was ready to move on to the next town, he'd sell them into human trafficking.

Bile rose up my throat as I thought about what could have happened to me had that motorcycle club not intervened when they had. I tried to force it down but, like most nights, I couldn't hold it in. Kicking the covers off, I dashed to the bathroom and skidded to my knees next to the toilet, throwing up everything I'd managed to eat for dinner.

The nightmares that tormented me when I slept weren't actually nightmares at all. They were snippets of memories returning to me. Horrible, erotic acts Godfrey and his men had forced me to do or forced on me. I'd been twenty-eight years old when my parents had died in a car accident and Godfrey had stepped in to *help* me. I should have been too old for him to set his sights on, but thanks to how I was raised, I'd been his perfect victim.

There were days I got so angry with my parents. Not for dying, although I did wish that had never happened. No, I was furious with them for raising me the way they had. I didn't even know why they'd done it. I'm sure I'd be able to handle it better if I'd known there had been a good reason behind them wanting me to stay their little girl forever. But they'd never told me why they did what they did. And now they were gone I couldn't ask.

They'd kept me innocent and naive of the world, sheltering me from just about everything. I'd never even left Rocky Gully before I'd been rescued, blissfully ignorant of how evil the world could be. I'd been childlike. A little girl in a woman's body. Looking back at my former self now, I could barely believe that person even existed. Going to school had given me a little reality to ground myself with, but that hadn't been enough to dispel everything my parents had ingrained in me and reinforced whenever I questioned anything. I'd only managed one year at high school before they'd pulled me out to homeschool me. They hadn't liked the questions I'd come home with.

They'd only ever shown me the good and sweet things of the world, they hadn't appreciated that the other kids at the high school seemed to be taking great pleasure in trying to educate me on the evils of the world. But even the other kids had never spoken to me about human trafficking, about how some men would take a person, train them, then sell them as a sex slave. I doubted I would have believed them if they had.

I swiped the tears from my cheeks and shifted to sit on the floor, leaning back against the tile wall, allowing the coldness seeping into me to ground me to the present.

Godfrey had me under his full control for ten months. He'd taken my virginity that first night he'd moved in after my parents' deaths. The memories from that evening were regular ones my nightmares forced me to relive. Him offering me tea to help calm me so I could sleep, then him telling me to strip when I told him I was getting hot. With a gag, I shifted forward to throw up again. He'd been cruel, saying horrible, dirty things as he'd gleefully taken my innocence. The promises he'd made... All the therapy in the world would never completely wash away all the dirt I now had within me. I doubt I'd ever be able to clean out my mind enough that I could live in peace again.

After I was rescued, I'd spent ten days in the hospital detoxing from the drug and getting physically healthy, then I'd moved here to this psychiatric clinic in Houston. I had a love-hate relationship with this place. I was safe here. I knew no one would come into my room at night and I could move around at will during the day. But I had to stay here, not that I wanted to go out into the city. It was big, loud and scary out there. But I couldn't go home, back to my job where I could earn the money I'd need to move forward. To be truly free.

My therapist assured me I'd get back to doing those things in time, but I wasn't ready. I had to focus on healing my mind, on processing and dealing with the memories as they returned. But I wasn't sure I believed her. I doubted I'd ever leave this place. Even though that poison might be out of my system, it had caused damage the doctors suspected could be permanent. There was no way to be positive because no one had ever documented side-effects or outcomes of prolonged use. I was the guinea pig in this case.

My main issue was that my short-term memory was a mess, and the doctors couldn't tell me if it would improve. I'd do things like forget I ate dinner and go to get it only to be told I'd already eaten. I'd find myself dressed and out in the game room with no recollection of how I'd gotten there. At least here where I was safe, I knew nothing horrible had happened during my missing time.

It was extremely frustrating. There were times it would overwhelm me, and I'd get so angry that I'd lash out. Then I'd be sedated, but they didn't like doing that. My therapist told me the sedatives were addictive and I was here to get better, not to find a new crutch to lean on. I had to agree with her. I'd just gotten free from one drug and had no desire to get hooked on any others.

A sharp pain to the back of my knee woke me. I tried to lift my head, frowning as I had no recollection of falling asleep, but realized I'd laid down on the tiled floor of the bathroom at some point. I swung my head to see what had stirred me. A bug of some kind, maybe? I gasped when I saw who stood there, with an empty needle in his hand.

"Hello, Mary. Remember me?"

The sound of the name Godfrey and his men always used when I'd been drugged had my heart racing. I parted my lips to scream but he clapped a palm over my mouth before I could make a sound.

"Uh, uh, uh. No screaming, baby girl. Maybe you don't remember me. Godfrey was going to wean you off the drug once he'd finished training you for me, so you'd remember who your master was. But those fuckers came and ruined everything before we got to that point."

My eyesight went wavy and my muscles turned to jelly as whatever he'd injected into me took hold. As I slumped back toward the floor, he shifted his grip, which thankfully prevented my head from cracking back against the tile.

"Time for you to come home, baby girl."

On second thought, I wish he'd let my head slam against the tile. With any luck, it would have killed me. As he lifted me and carried me from my room, I was mentally screaming but my body was useless, my vocal cords numb, so no sound left my mouth. A tear trailed from my eye around to my ear as I realized I was going straight back to hell and this time Elizabeth and her Charon MC weren't around to come to my rescue.

Keys
Monday morning church was normally brief and mainly

covered who was going to work where in the coming week. Scout hadn't mentioned the security business idea yet and as things wound down, I worried he'd either forgotten or hadn't been serious about the idea. Surely, he wouldn't have said it just to placate me. At the moment where he'd normally end things, I glanced over at him with a raised eyebrow. He gave me a nod and I relaxed, realizing he hadn't even reached for his gavel and intended on bringing up the idea as the final piece of club business.

"Shut the fuck up and sit down, we ain't done."

The men, who'd all been getting ready to leave, sat again and went silent.

"We're going to be establishing another business. This one is a big step for the club, and it's long overdue. We all know how Keys has been our eye in the sky for-fucking-ever. His vigilance has saved all of us at some point or another, along with many of those we hold dear. But it's too big a job for one man. Bridgewater is growing, as is our club. We need a team to step up and help Keys out. It'll be an official business and you'll get paid for the work, but don't offer your services lightly. You'll be required to work both night and day shifts, and you'll see things you need to keep to your fucking self. Most importantly, you'll not only have access to very private information on a lot of people, but the means to track and watch basically anyone in town. You need to make a vow to the club that you will not abuse that access. Keys will train the team and you'll be given all the support you need. You'll report directly to Keys, or if he's off grid for some reason, to me. I'll give you all a few minutes to think on it."

He stayed silent as he looked around the room and I did the same thing. As the club secretary, I was sitting at the table beside Scout and the other officers, so it was easy to take in the faces of the club brothers. They all looked serious and I could see a few sitting up straighter, like they wanted to step up.

Scout turned to me before he spoke again. "You thought of a name for this thing yet?"

I grinned as I sat back in my seat. Donna and I had tossed around several ideas but had both made the same choice of name in the end.

"Athena Security and Protection Services."

Scout nodded. "Sticking with the Greek thing. I like it."

Mac leaned forward to get my attention. "Why Athena? She's not some fucked-up river or something, right?"

I chuckled. I'd heard Mac had questioned why we'd named the club's bar Styx.

"Athena was the goddess of wisdom and warfare, and handicrafts. So, things like reason, skill, peace, intelligence and battle strategy all come under her guard. Donna helped me pick out the name and I think it's perfect."

Mac gave me a nod before he sat back. "Sounds good, brother."

Scout also nodded before he turned back to the rest of the club. "Right. You've all had your chance to think this shit over. Those who want to join the team stay behind, everyone else can get going."

He slammed the gavel. "Church is over."

When Taz unlocked the door, it was pulled from his grip and before he knew what was going on, he had Donna in his arms as she tried to rush into the room.

"Whoa, darlin', you know you're not allowed in here."

I stood fast enough my chair crashed behind me at the pained look on my woman's face. Donna knew the rules. She wouldn't ever try to gain access without a damn good reason.

"Let her through, Taz. Donna, what happened?" Scout's voice once more silenced everyone.

"Mirabelle's been taken."

I rushed around the table to get to Donna. "What do you mean?"

"Somehow we switched phones this morning. I didn't realize I had yours until it rang and I answered it."

I shook my head. "That doesn't matter, who called? What did they say?"

"She wouldn't give me her name, but she works at the facility in Houston. She said that in the early hours of this morning a man broke in and took Mirabelle. We have to find her."

"What about Tabitha? And her brother, Todd? Are they all right?"

Donna looked to Arrow and I could see the sheen of tears in her eyes. "Mirabelle was the only one taken."

I pulled her in against me to comfort her and looked

over her head to Scout, then around the room.

"Baptism by fire, brothers. Those who want to be part of Athena Security and Protection Services, grab your laptops, tablets, phones... whatever tech you have here at the clubhouse and meet me in my office. We have a missing woman to track."

Chapter 12

Keys

Scout had rung the facility to get more information while I'd come into my office to set up my laptop to start tracing Mirabelle's tracker. Without anyone's knowledge or approval, I'd injected Mirabelle, Todd and Tabitha with a small tracking chip. At some point during the night of their rescue all three had been in the tank getting medical treatment and I'd been able to make the insertions quickly. Todd had been unconscious at the time, Mirabelle high on the shit Godfrey had given her and Tabitha had been too focused on her brother to notice what was being done to her. So now they all had a tiny chip inside them that I could tap into at will. The chips were my own creation, and this was the first time I'd had the chance to test how well they functioned. I fucking prayed it worked as well as I hoped.

Logging into the system, I set it running to track Mirabelle's chip, then moved to set up the devices the others had so they could start reviewing the video feeds from the facility to see if we could work out who the fuck had taken her. When Scout tried to come in, he struggled to find room.

"We're going to need to find somewhere with more space to run this thing."

I nodded. "What did you find out?"

"First up, please tell me you found a way to tag her before she went into that place."

I gave him a shit-eating grin. "Sure as fuck did. Tagged all three of them, but none of them know about it. I've also hacked into the feeds at that psych facility they're all staying at too, and that's what I have everyone going over. See if we can identify who took her. What info did you get?"

"Not much. They didn't notice she was gone until this morning because they don't do nighttime checks on her. After what Godfrey did to her, she can't handle having people in the room while she's sleeping. They tried early on to monitor her, but she always woke up and freaked out when her door was opened, let alone if someone entered. They shouldn't be telling us details, but since we pay the bill, they used that as an excuse to update us. The cops have been informed but they won't do shit. And the staff knows it. They know as well as we do that we're that girl's only chance. Especially since the cops have already indicated that since Maribelle's an adult, she has every right to check herself out. They seem to be happy to ignore the fact she didn't fucking check herself out, but just up and vanished in the night."

I shook my head. No way was that girl ready to be out

on her own. Not after all that was done to her. She was twenty-eight going on ten, mentally. Her folks had raised her to always be their little girl. She had no skills to combat a predator like Godfrey coming after her, or to deal with the aftermath of what he'd forced on her.

"What about the other two? Todd and Tabitha, the brother and sister. Donna said they weren't taken, but were they harmed at all?"

Scout turned to Arrow and gave him a nod. "They were both safely in their rooms. Neither mentioned seeing or hearing anything unusual during the night."

I was glad at least those two were fine but I had serious concerns for Maribelle, and I knew Donna would be out of her mind with worry for the woman. She hadn't been sure how Mirabelle would cope with the facility in the first place, but there hadn't been any other option for her.

"What will you do when you find Mirabelle?"

Donna stood at the doorway, her arms crossed over her chest, looking about as heartbroken as a woman could. Scout looked to me before focusing back on my woman while I went back to my laptop to see if we had a location yet.

"That depends on where we find her and what state she's in. When we rescued her from Godfrey, she became club property. We will make sure she's safe and well cared for, wherever she ends up."

Out the corner of my eye, I saw the way she held Scout's gaze. She was scared for Mirabelle, but she wasn't going to back down. Her inner momma bear had been woken and she wouldn't stop until that woman had been found and taken care of.

"I can't just sit on the sidelines with this one, Scout. I can't allow another woman to die at Godfrey's hands. And even though this isn't him in person, I know in my gut, this is connected to him. And that man makes Sledge look like a little kitten by comparison."

Scout rested a hand on each of Donna's shoulders, cutting off her words.

"Sugar, no one doubts for a moment that you'll be in the tank with your man when we go to get her. The club owes you as much as we owe Keys with all the rescues you perform. Keys gets us the information, you help us patch up the victims. And us. The club is indebted to you both, and we would *never* prevent you from coming on a run with us in the tank. You don't even need to ask."

She nodded, blinking really fast as though she were trying not to cry.

"Go sit out in the main area, get a prospect to get you a bottle of water and try to relax. We need you at one hundred percent and ready to go the moment we have a location, okay?"

I hated that I couldn't go with Donna and comfort her. Hopefully once I got this team trained and running, I would be able to do just that. Although not with cases like this, that I was personally involved with.

Godfrey had been an evil son of a bitch who'd pretended to be a pastor while he'd taken in teens and adults alike to abuse and turn into sex slaves that he would then sell off once he was done with them. When we'd busted open his house of horrors, we'd found three victims. Mirabelle had been in an upstairs room, naked and high on a new date-rape type drug we'd come across before, being raped by two of Godfrey's men.

Todd, a teenage boy, had been in the basement, being tortured in front of Bess, Needles' old lady. His sister, Tabitha, had been found upstairs cleaning the house. She'd had a fucking shock collar on and had been unaware that Godfrey held her brother. He'd told her Todd had died months earlier.

The whole situation was horrific and all three of them had needed medical attention. Although Tabitha hadn't been drugged at all from what we could tell, she'd still been horribly abused. Donna and I had been stretched to our limit that night to get all three sorted enough we could transport them to hospital. But we'd done it.

Both the women were doing better than Todd, who was still near catatonic. The torture and abuse he'd suffered was just too much for his young mind to cope with and he'd shut down. Honestly, I had no fucking idea if he'd ever recover, but I was sure his sister's recovery depended on his. She blamed herself for his being taken in the first place and was one hundred percent about seeing her brother get better. From the start, she'd pushed away any attempts to assist her, assuring everyone she was fine and her brother was the one they should focus on.

Donna had voiced her concern to me more than once

that she was worried the facility was going to force Mirabelle's discharge, and I had to agree with her. At some point they would conclude they couldn't help her if she refused to accept it. That if she was truly as fine as she said she was, she didn't need them. That young woman was not okay in the least. I looked to Arrow, who was focused completely on his task of going through video footage. From the first, Arrow had taken an interest in Tabitha, and I knew she had a champion in him. He'd never let her fall. Although I did worry on how she'd react to my brother's interest in her after the abuse she'd suffered.

"Got something."

I moved to look over Arrow's shoulder as he rewound the footage to show Scout and me what he'd found. He'd been delegated the cameras in the hallway outside of Mirabelle's room to go through. Arrow stopped and hit play as a man strode confidently down the middle of the hallway. He was in the uniform all the staff wore but there was something about him I didn't like. We all silently watched as he entered Maribelle's room. I glanced to the time stamp that read 22:18. When he didn't come straight back out, Arrow sped things up until the door began to open, then he slowed it back down. The others echoed my curse when the man reappeared with a limp Mirabelle in his arms. The time stamp was now at 22:34.

"Bastard took her from her room at ten thirty last night. He's had her a full twelve hours."

"You get a clear shot of the fucker's face?"

Arrow proved he was a fast learner and rewound it again until he could snatch a screen grab of his face.

"What do I need to do with it, Keys?"

I guided him through the process of loading the image into my facial recognition program.

"And now we wait for it to do its thing."

Leaving Arrow to keep watching the search, I returned to my laptop to see if it had locked in on Mirabelle's location yet, making a mental note that I needed to work on the program's speed. The teething issues on new tech were always a bitch and without fail would crop up at the worst possible times. When the trace finally came through, I sighed in relief.

"Okay, got a location." I plugged the coordinates into the satellite system I had access to and winced at the result. "Ah, fuck. She's about an hour north of Rocky Gully, in Riverton, the town where Godfrey was set up in before he moved down there. This has to be linked to him."

Scout frowned but stayed standing strong. "Send the address around, then I'm going to need you and Donna in the tank. Keg, you drive so Keys can stay in contact with Arrow. See if we can get a name on this fucker before we get there. Tiny, you and Eagle take a van for the garbage. Everyone else, get ready to ride."

With his orders given, he turned to head out of the room. I texted the address to everyone then gathered up my laptop and phone and went to find Donna. We then headed out the front to our baby, the tank.

"I'll hop in the back so you can sit up the front and direct Keg."

I gave her a hard, fast kiss before she turned to open the rear of the van and got in, I shut the doors behind her. I headed to the front seat to get myself settled and ready to roll. Keg hopped up behind the wheel and I tossed him the keys. The roar of all the Harleys coming to life around us had me smiling even under the dire circumstances.

"Nothing beats that sound, does it?"

Keg chuckled. "Nope. Only thing missing is us out there on our machines, adding to the symphony."

"Ain't that the truth. But we'll have the most important job of all once we arrive. We get to be the ones who ride out with the damsel in distress safely with us."

Keg scoffed. "You been reading fairytales, Keys? Is that what you really do when you have your nose pressed up against your laptop? You reading about Prince fucking Charming and his princess?"

I laughed as he took off and followed the bikes out of the compound and toward Riverton. "Sure, brother. You got me. I'm addicted to a good happily ever after."

That even received a chuckle from Donna sitting in the rear. The closer we got to the location, the tenser I became. Mirabelle's marker hadn't moved at all and I started praying the girl was still alive. I wasn't sure I could handle failing someone else at the moment, not when I was just managing to crawl out from under all the guilt I was already carrying. When we hit the driveway of the house she was in, the bikes parted to either side of the road to let us through.

"Your lucky day, Keg. You get to take out the gate."

"Yeehaw, motherfucker!"

I shut my laptop and stowed it as I called out for Donna to hold on to something. She'd have her seat belt on, same as Keg and me, but taking out a metal gate was going to give us all a solid jolt. The reason we called this beast a tank and not a bus was due to the armored plating on the outside. This thing was a bulletproof machine that could go pretty much anywhere. On the front was a bull bar that had been reinforced to the point it could knock down a damn house if we wanted to. It'd handle this asshole's gate with no trouble. This wasn't the first time we'd used it as a battering ram, and I doubted it'd be the last.

"Hang on to your hats, here we go!"

I chuckled as I hung onto the oh-shit handle. Keg sounded way too excited about getting to plow through the barrier, but I understood how he felt. There was something exhilarating about driving this beast through a locked gate. Especially when you knew the place was owned by an asshole you intended to send straight to hell once you caught up with him.

Mirabelle

I had no idea what this bastard had dosed me up on but was grateful it was finally beginning to wear off. I flexed my fingers, one at a time, until I could move them all, then I wriggled my toes. I was up to testing my elbows and knees when I heard a terrible crash and screeching from outside. There was also a dull roar I'd heard once before. A roar that grew louder and made me want to weep in relief, even as I struggled to believe I was really hearing the sound.

The club had come. Somehow, they'd known I'd been taken, and they'd come. Tears blurred my vision as I held my breath and forced my body to work, to sit up on the bed I was on. I winced when I glanced down and caught an eyeful of what he'd dressed me in earlier.

As soon as we'd arrived here, he'd cut my pajamas off and dressed me in lacy panties and a baby-doll-style nightie. He'd even taken the time to put my blonde curls into pig tails. He kept calling me baby girl and the more he did, the more I realized that was what he wanted from me. For me to be like a small child, but no doubt one he could also use for sex.

A shudder ran through me as I recalled what he'd promised would happen once the drug wore off. How he didn't have the drug Godfrey had used so he hoped I remembered all my lessons because he'd be putting my training to good use real soon.

Closing my eyes, I prayed those loud motorcycles close by were the club that had saved me before. I couldn't go through what he'd told me would happen. I wasn't strong enough. Licking my dry lips, I looked around at all the frilly girlie stuff around the room. White teddy bears sat piled on a shelf, and the dresser had pots of hair ties and other things a young girl would love. There was so much pink around me, it hurt my eyes.

Forcing my body to move again, I stood on shaky legs, but I refused to go down. I had to get out of here. If those bikes weren't the club, they were at least a distraction that could allow me my only chance at escape. Because if I couldn't get free, I'd die trying. I would not stay here and willingly be this man's plaything.

I made it to the door but when I tried to open it, it wouldn't budge. I was locked in.

"No!"

I grabbed the handle and rattled the hell out of it, frustrated that I couldn't manage to open it.

"Okay, Maribelle. Time to calm down and think this through. Panic won't get you anywhere."

Taking a few deep, calming breaths, I relaxed enough to think. The door was a no go, which left the windows as my only other exit option. My legs were thankfully less shaky as I strode over and shoved the curtain aside to look out the clean glass. I squeezed my eyes shut when I noticed I was not on the ground level but one story up.

"That's okay. It's not that far. I can do this."

I shoved the window all the way open and leaned out, only to groan when I saw the rose bushes below. Why couldn't I catch a damn break? I tightened my grip on the window ledge as I contemplated what to do. Could I jump far enough out to miss the roses? How much would it hurt if I did? The grass that lay further out wasn't exactly the thickest looking lawn around. When the door behind me rattled and started to open I made my decision. Any damage I got from jumping would be better than whatever that man had planned for me.

I'd just wait to see who came through the door before I leapt. It might be the club. Lord, I prayed it was the club. Tears tracked down my cheeks, but I ignored them as I stared at the door. It opened to reveal my nightmare had returned. Dammit. Taking a deep breath, I turned my attention back to climbing up onto the window ledge to take my chances with the roses.

"Whoa! Mary, stop! What are you doing?"

I glanced over at him, recalling his face suddenly. Greg Simmons. He'd often come in the evenings to speak with Godfrey. He seemed frozen in shock that I would try to escape him. "I'd rather die in the roses than live as your plaything."

He shook his head and took a step toward me. I shifted my grip and was about to leap when a noise had me glancing one more time behind me. A large man I'd seen before came looming up behind Greg and with a fast move, the Charon MC man slammed the butt of his gun against Greg's head and he crumpled to the ground, unconscious.

Blinking, I tried to process what had just happened. Had it been real? Or had I lost my mind and imagined it all? My heart rate ticked up and suddenly I was struggling to breathe. I fell away from the window, dropping to my hands and knees on the thick carpet as a panic attack took me over.

"Hey, Maribelle, you're okay. You're safe now."

Closing my eyes, I let my body collapse on the floor. The club was here. I was safe.

"Tiny, take that trash out to the van, would you? She doesn't need to be seeing him ever again. We'll deal with him later. Eagle, find her something more to wear. Motherfucking asshole."

A large hand on my back had me jerking and shuffling away from the contact, up against the wall. There was a cool breeze in the room. The window was open. Why was the window open? I looked up into the bearded face of a man I'd seen before.

"Hey, honey, it's okay. Not sure if you remember me from last time, but I'm Scout, the president of the Charon MC. We came to rescue you, again. I've got Donna and Keys out in the ambulance waiting to check you over, then we'll get out of here. Take you back to Houston."

I'd lost some memory again, dammit. I knew Greg had come and taken me from Houston, but how had I ended up here? With the club?

"Not Houston. It's not safe there. Please don't take me back there."

He nodded before he responded. "Fair enough. For now, we'll head back to our clubhouse. How's that sound? We'll get a few of the old ladies to come in to keep you company while we work out what's best for you."

I looked down at the skimpy nightgown I was wearing. "I can't see anyone like this."

"Don't you worry, we'll get you something to change into before anyone will see you."

A tall man who had to be Native American with his angular features and long black hair came up and handed Scout a t-shirt. Considering the fact his chest was bare under his leather vest, I guessed it was his.

"Sorry, Prez, ain't nothing here that's any better than what she's got on. Take my shirt for now. I'll message Silk to get her something for when we get back."

Kneeling in front of me, Scout held the shirt out. "C'mon, honey, let's get this on you so we can get you out of this place."

I reached out and took the shirt, pulling it over my head and threading my arms through the sleeves before I took Scout's hand, allowing him to help me to stand.

"We know he drugged you with something when he took you. Can you walk or do you want me to carry you?"

I took a step to confirm my legs were still solid before I voiced my assurance to Scout.

"It seems to have worn off now. I can walk."

With a nod, he held his arm out to indicate I should walk in front of him. The man with the gorgeous long hair took the lead while the other men who'd come into the room followed behind us. I was surrounded by big, tough, armed men and I'd never felt safer. I just prayed that this time the feeling would last.

Chapter 13

Donna

I held my breath as the men filed out of the house, Eagle in the lead. I frowned when I noticed he no longer had a shirt on under his cut. Out on a job, that usually meant someone else was wearing it. I shuddered as images of why Maribelle would need his shirt flickered in my mind, until Eagle moved out of the way to reveal her. She looked a little shaky on her feet, but she was walking unaided with Scout right behind her, ready to catch her if she did fall. We'd already pulled the gurney out so when she was close enough, I held my hand out to her.

"Hi, Maribelle. Not sure if you remember me from last time, but I'm Donna. I'm a registered nurse and will take good care of you, okay?"

She gave me a small nod, and after trying to tug Eagle's shirt down to cover more of her legs, she took my hand. I guided her to sit, then lay on the gurney and Keys was fast to get a blanket over her as soon as her back hit the mattress.

"We're just going to get you loaded into the back of the

bus, okay? It'll give us some privacy. After we get you settled in, we'll head on back to—"

She stiffened and Scout cut me off from saying anything more. "We're taking her back to the clubhouse. She'll be safe there."

Eagle had his phone out as he spoke up next. "I'm texting Silk to sort out some clothes for you to wear, darlin'."

"A shower?"

Her voice was quiet, like she wasn't sure if she had permission to speak.

"Sure thing, sugar. We'll get you settled into one of the rooms upstairs. They lock and each have their own bathrooms. You'll be completely safe to have as long a shower as you like. Then once you're ready, you can join us downstairs and we'll sort out what you want to do next."

She didn't look injured, no blood that I could see, or even bruises. I prayed we'd been in time to prevent her from being raped.

Once she was inside the tank and I'd climbed in beside her, Keys shut the doors and we had a little privacy.

"Mirabelle, I need to ask some things you probably don't want to talk about. I promise I won't share what you tell me with anyone outside a doctor if you need one. Did he hurt you in any way? Touch you inappropriately?"

Tears glazed over her cornflower blue eyes before she blinked them away. "He came into my room and drugged me with something that made it so I couldn't move. I can't remember the car ride at all, but I don't think he did anything to me while we were traveling. When we got here, he changed my clothes. He—" She paused to take a breath, then cleared her throat. I grabbed a bottle of water and cracked the seal for her, helping her sit up so she could take a few mouthfuls of the cool liquid. "He touched me. After he cut my clothes off. But he said he wanted me to be able to move and respond to him before he'd *fuck* me."

I could tell Mirabelle wasn't used to swearing. She'd probably never really even heard curse words much, let alone used them in the past. If she wanted to stay at the clubhouse, that would change quickly.

"Okay, honey. Drink some more water. That's it. Do you hurt anywhere? Inside or out, you can tell me anything. I'm here to help you any way I can."

She shook her head and picked at the label on the bottle. "I just feel dirty. I want out of this stupid thing he put on me and—" She handed me the bottle in a rush and ripped at the hair ties that were holding her hair into two pigtails, like a little girl would wear. Once she had them free, she threw them away from her. "He called me his baby girl."

Her respiration rate increased quickly as she got more and more worked up. I needed to get her calm so we could get out of here. I knew Keys was waiting outside the rear door for my signal we were ready to go and to confirm she didn't need a hospital. Setting the water bottle aside, I took her hands in mine.

"It's all over now, Mirabelle. He'll never get to you

again. The club will make sure of it."

She shifted her gaze to look me in the eye. "How can they?"

I smiled gently at her. "The Charon MC is known for taking care of those it considers its own. After we rescued you from Godfrey, you joined that group. You can always call on the club to come to your aide. Hang on a sec, let me tell Keys we're ready to go, then I'll explain it in more detail."

I moved to open the rear door and smiled at Keys who stood guard, waiting. "Hey, babe, we're good to go. No need for the hospital, so just back to the clubhouse."

He leaned in and stole a quick kiss before he strode off toward the front of the vehicle while I reclosed the door and shifted to get Mirabelle ready for the drive. Once I was buckled into my own seat, I continued to tell her about the club, without coming out and saying what they'd do to her kidnapper.

"Did you ever study Greek mythology?"

She shook her head. "My parents wouldn't have let me even if I'd wanted to. There was no room in their lives for other cultures."

My heart hurt for this woman. Her parents had sheltered her so much from the world, she'd had no sense of self-preservation when they'd died and left her open to its darker side. Godfrey must have thought he'd hit the jackpot when he'd found her.

"Well, in Greek mythology they didn't have Heaven or Hell, they had the Elysian Fields for the souls of the good and worthy, and Hades for the souls filled with evil. To gain entrance to either one, a departed soul needed to cross a river on the ferry. The Charon was the name of the ferryman. It was he alone who would decide where a soul would spend eternity. It's after that ferryman that the Charon MC was named. They take people like yourself— a good, honest woman—and they decide they need to protect you. That you deserve all the good things in life. While they take someone like your kidnapper, and they pass judgement on him and send him for his eternal rest with all the other evil souls. Do you understand what I'm saying?"

She nodded. "He deserves whatever happens to him and more. He *bought* me."

I saw Keys turn his head slightly to hear her better and I knew he wanted to know more. So did I. I wanted all the information we could get so they could take it out of that asshole's hide before they killed him.

"What do you mean?"

"He told me that Godfrey was training me for him. That once he was ready to leave Rocky Gully, he'd deliver me to Greg. That's his name. Greg Simmons. I remember him often coming around in the evening for Bible study sessions with Godfrey." A shudder ran through her body as she closed her eyes for a few moments. "My nightmares revealed the truth behind that lie. What they did had nothing at all to do with the Bible. No matter how many times they called me Mary or referred to Tabitha as Martha."

"They gave you new names?"

"Well, Mary is sort of an abbreviation of Maribelle, and they only used it when I was drugged. Godfrey liked to have me by his feet, worshiping him while he had Tabitha running around doing all the chores. You know… like the Bible story about Mary and Martha? I honestly didn't know Tabitha wasn't named Martha until after we were rescued."

Tears streamed down her face and I reached over and rested my hand on her forearm, wishing I could do more to comfort her. "That's over with now, Maribelle. We will make sure you're always safe from here on out."

I knew I shouldn't make that promise—that it wasn't my place to do so—but I couldn't help it. This might be a woman lying before me, but she was basically a child. Her parents had done her a great disservice, then Godfrey and his drugs had further compounded the issue. We never should have let her leave Bridgewater and the safety net the Charon MC provided to the town.

Keys

Once we arrived at the clubhouse, I told the women to wait in the tank while I got out and made sure the front room had been cleared out so no one would see Maribelle until she was ready to be seen.

"How's she doing?"

I gave a Scout a nod. "We got there before he raped her,

but not before he got his hands on her. She wants a shower and to clean up before anyone else sees her."

"Fair enough." Scout looked around. "Keg and Mac, go make sure the way is clear for us to get her upstairs. Eagle? Go find Silk and see what she's set up for her."

I grabbed Scout's shoulder before he could take off inside. "She told Donna his name was Greg Simmons, that he'd bought her from Godfrey. He was supposed to take delivery after the fuck was done training her and was ready to move on from Rocky Gully."

The growl that came from Scout had me jerking my hand away from him in reflex. "We'd guessed that was what he was planning to do, but to have it confirmed? Makes me wish it was possible to kill a man more than once."

I huffed out a breath. "Couldn't agree more. We might need to pass Greg on to the feds so they can use him to trace others Godfrey has sold."

Scout shook his head. "Not this time. We'll see what we can get out of him and if we can find the victims, we'll go rescue them ourselves. The feds have their hands tied with this shit. And I don't want to risk having that fucker back out on the streets."

I nodded, happy with his decision. "That's my thought too, but I had to play the devil's advocate there for a moment. Needed to be sure we considered all the options."

Scout clapped me on the back. "We're good, brother. You're right to make sure we look at things from all angles. And we have handed over shit to the feds in the past, but this time I'm not willing to let them handle it. They should have already found Greg and dealt with him. I'm sure they would have found something linking back to him in all of Godfrey's records. I'm not fucking happy they've not investigated as deeply as they should have."

"I didn't get a chance to swipe a copy of Godfrey's hard drive when we raided his place, want me to get the new team on getting a hold of it?"

"Yeah, talk to Flick. She might have some ideas on how you'll be able to get it. If the feds have missed this guy, you know they've missed others. There could be buyers out there waiting for a chance to grab Tabitha and Todd. We need to know."

Silk came out, ending our conversation, not that we needed to say any more. Scout knew I didn't want to have to look at all the depraved shit Godfrey had been into, but for the sake of the safety of his victims I would do it. At least with the new team, it wasn't solely on my shoulders.

"We've got one of the rooms upstairs all set up for her. Clean clothes in the closet, girlie shit in the bathroom. It's all set to go."

"Thanks, Silk, could you head on back to the kitchen for now? Once the front room is empty, we'll get her inside and up the stairs. She doesn't want to see anyone till she's had a chance to wash up and change."

Silk gave Scout a nod. "Fair enough. Let me know if I can do anything else."

"Could you call in Mercedes, Veronica and Bess? Have

them here to talk with her when she's ready for it."

I liked how Scout was thinking. Mercedes had been raised in a cult, Veronica had been groomed and abused by her uncle and Bess had been taken by Godfrey. She'd been the reason we found out about him and went in to end his bullshit. Together with Donna, the women would be the perfect support group for Mirabelle.

"Sure, I'll go make the calls."

Moments after she'd gone through the door, Mac came back out. "It's clear, get Donna to bring her in."

I cracked open the rear door and helped Donna hop down before she turned to help Maribelle. Once she was standing, Donna wrapped the blanket from the gurney around her and started guiding her toward the clubhouse. Scout opened the door and closed it firmly behind them before he turned toward the van.

"Right, let's make the most of everyone being out of the main rooms to get this piece of shit down to the basement. Tiny, he awake yet? You didn't kill him already did you, brother?"

"Nah, he's still breathing, Prez. I only hit the fucker the once back at the house. I'm sure he'll be awake and ready to answer your questions by nightfall."

Scout grinned but it wasn't a happy smile. More like one the devil wore just before he struck. "Excellent. He'll be good to go by the time we've got Maribelle settled in." He rolled his shoulders. "Been a minute since I got to work over a fucker who deserved it as much as this asshole does."

As Tiny went and dragged the bastard out of the van and carried him inside, I turned to Scout again. "I don't think it's wise to have her living here, Prez. Fuck, brother, I didn't know a woman could be that innocent in this day and age. It's like her parents kept her under a rock or something."

Scout nodded, a frown marring his brow. "Yeah, she'll never cope staying here long-term, and it sure as fuck won't help her heal to see what goes on here once the whores have free rein of the place in the evenings. You got any ideas, I'm all ears."

We moved inside with the others and after grabbing drinks from the bar, sat at one of the tables. Donna came to sit beside me, and I pulled her in close enough that I could wrap my arm around her shoulders.

"I can't see her ever agreeing to return to the facility in Houston. Now she's been snatched from there, she won't ever feel safe there. I haven't spoken to Donna about it, but maybe we could take her in."

I'd seen the look in my woman's eyes. She'd told Mirabelle the club had claimed her as one of ours, but in reality it was Donna who'd claimed that woman. Donna would be that woman's momma bear and beat off anyone who even thought of causing her harm.

Scout and I both looked to Donna as she blinked up at us in shock at what I'd suggested.

"What do you say, Donna? You and Keys want to take on guardianship of this woman?"

"Um, well, of course we'll do whatever we can to help

her. I'm not sure our current place is suitable though, it only has the one bathroom. She'll need her own space."

Scout leaned forward and Donna stopped speaking.

"The house on the other side of the road from us has just hit the market. Four bedrooms, two and a half baths. Might be good to have a fresh start in a new place for all three of you. And you'll be on the same street with the rest of us. Lots of the club close by to help out if needed."

With that, he moved to stand. "I'll leave you to think about it. Just let me know what you wanna do. If you feel you can't take her in, we'll sort out something else for her."

He walked away and Donna shifted on the seat so she faced me. "What do you think? A new home, one not filled with memories might be good for us. Being closer to the others would be nice."

I looked into my woman's face and nodded. "Yeah, they say a change is as good as a holiday, don't they? We can at least go check this place out. See if we like it."

"We need to talk with Mirabelle, too. She needs to have a say in where she's going to live."

"Absolutely. We'll have a chat with her when she comes down. Maybe get her to come with us to check out the new house."

"And, Keys? I still want my weekend away with you. But it can wait until we have Mirabelle settled."

With a smile, she leaned in for a kiss and setting my drink aside, I tangled my fingers in her hair and brought her mouth to mine so I could kiss her deeply like I wanted to. I was grateful and happy that we were back on track together and moving forward from the past.

Mirabelle

I was surprised how clean and tidy the clubhouse was. The room they gave me was small but had all the necessities. A basic closet with built-in shelves, chair, double bed and small bathroom with my own shower and toilet. It was everything I needed, especially since the door had a lock on it. I was sure others had a key, but the chair fit under the handle and gave me another layer of safety.

I didn't bother taking more than a glance at everything before I went straight for the bathroom and turned the taps on. I carefully took off the shirt I'd been given, then roughly pulled the disgusting nightie and panties off. I tried to rip them up but when I couldn't, I satisfied myself with shoving them into the pedal-operated trash bin and letting the lid slam closed on it.

Stepping under the water, I was surprised to see the line-up of girlie products on the rack hanging from the shower head. When I noticed every one of them was brand new, I decided not to worry about why or how they got here and picked up the body wash to flip it open and take a sniff. Instantly, the calming scent of lavender surrounded me and with a smile, I put it back and picked up the shampoo. After washing my hair and putting some conditioner through it, I grabbed the body wash again, along with the shower puff and set about scrubbing every inch of my body. Wanting—no, needing—to get every bit of Greg's filth off me.

By the time I stepped out of the shower, my skin was pink, but I didn't care. I felt one hundred times better than I had before. Wrapping a towel around my hair and another around my body, I headed back out into the room. After checking the chair was still in place under the doorknob, I headed over to the closet, hoping the man who'd said he was going to text someone about getting me clothes had done so. No way was I going to be heading anywhere wearing only a towel.

A sticky note was on the door of the closet.

"Everything is new and bought just for you. I hope you find something you like. Silk."

My eyes stung as I slid open the door to see several things neatly folded on the middle shelf. I wasn't sure what to do with this kindness. These were bikers and their wives. People my parents would never in a million years have allowed me to associate with, yet they were bending over backward to help me. For the second time. And I didn't know why. I couldn't repay them in any way, and so far, no one had said a thing about me paying for anything. Donna had explained the club did this for people it considered under its protection. But how did I earn that?

Considering the way Godfrey and others who my daddy and momma had praised, had treated me, I wasn't about to judge the Charon MC by my parents' moral compass. This whole experience had really made me sit back and think about the world and how so many judged people by appearance alone, and how wrong that was. It was what was within a person that really counted.

Blowing a breath, I wiped my eyes and reached in to shift through the clothing until I found something I'd be comfortable in. A pair of jeans that were soft, along with a pretty blue sweater that would cover up most of me beneath its fabric looked like a good choice. There was also a pair of pink panties with a pretty, lacy edging on them, and a stretchy sports bra, both with the tags still attached. Everything fit and once I was dressed, I reached in to grab the slip-on flats to put on before I returned to the bathroom to brush out my hair. Someone had left a hairdryer for me and I used it to dry off my curls. Leaving them loose around my face, I put everything away and looked at myself in the mirror for a few moments.

I looked exactly the same as I had before my parents had died, but I felt like a completely different person. Godfrey's crimes had changed me, almost broke me. But I'd survived. I was here and alive and maybe with the club's help, I could change again. Become someone new that I wanted to be. Something more than a victim.

With a deep breath, I left the bathroom and headed over to the door. Shifting the chair, I unlocked it and stalled out. Where was I supposed to go once I was ready? I couldn't remember what Donna had told me.

"Mirabelle?"

Relief washed over me and I opened the door to see Donna was waiting there for me.

"The other ladies have arrived and can't wait to meet you. You ready to head down?"

Ah, that's right. I was supposed to go downstairs to meet up with a few of the wives. I was glad Donna had come up to get me. I didn't even care if she'd done it because she knew I had memory issues. They were part of who I was now, and I needed to adjust to living with it. I wished I could keep Donna close. I already liked her a lot. She was calming to be around and had a way of smoothly helping me without bringing attention to the problem.

"That'd be great."

She waited for me to close and lock my door before walking beside me down the stairs.

"Like both of us, every one of the women downstairs has been through something traumatic, so you don't need to worry about them understanding or judging you. We're all survivors and only want to help you."

Wide-eyed in shock, I looked over at her, unable to believe someone so... well... normal, could have suffered like I had. She chuckled softly.

"I've come to realize almost everyone has suffered in some way or another. Life is not for the faint of heart. I think the club attracts those of us that have had someone try to break us. We can see that we fit here, that we'll find the understanding and support we need to keep going, to grow into who we want to be. I hope you find that here too."

I rested a hand on her arm and stopped walking. She stilled as well and turned to face me.

"You're really not going to take me back to Houston?"

Her expression softened. "Only if that's what you want. You're an adult, Mirabelle. You get to make the choice here. I know Scout offered for you to stay here as long as you liked, and that offer is still there. But I don't believe this is the best place for you. In the evenings it can get pretty wild and I'm worried that'll trigger your memories."

My heart sank at her words. This was my only option. But before I could say anything, she held her palm up to stop me.

"Don't panic. I have another option for you, but again, this is totally your choice and you can take as much time as you need to decide on what you want to do. Keys and I would like you to consider moving in with us. Our current place is a little cramped but we're going to be looking at a new house soon that is much bigger. You'd have your own room and bathroom, and as much privacy as you want, but with us close by to help you with anything you need."

Tears pricked my eyes again and my throat closed up, clogged with emotion. I didn't know what to say so I didn't even try. Instead, I leaned into the older woman and resting my head on her shoulder, hugged her.

"Oh, sweetheart."

She held me to her, running a palm over my hair and

instantly I felt calmer. Donna's maternal actions were soothing the ragged edges Godfrey and his friends had left on my soul. I didn't need time to decide, I knew where I wanted to be.

Pulling away, I wiped my eyes and smiled at her. "I'd love to take you up on your offer. But I can't be a charity case, I need to work."

Donna indicated I start walking down the stairs and once I started moving, she spoke again.

"I can understand that. Scout's wife, Marie, owns a cafe here in town. She's not here but one of the ladies who is, Mercedes, works for her. I'm sure we can sort out some type of job there, assuming you want to keep doing what you were before?"

I nodded. "For now, yes. But I think maybe one day I'd like to go back to school and study. Maybe be a therapist or something. I want to help other people."

Donna grinned at me and my heart warmed at the look of pride in her eyes.

"That sounds wonderful. You let me know when you're ready to start and we'll help you get it all sorted out. Now, let's get you introduced to the other old ladies."

"Old ladies?"

Donna smiled. "It's what bikers call their women. It basically means wife, although some of the brothers don't actually marry their old ladies. You'll get used to the slang the club uses in no time."

I allowed Donna to lead me over to a table surrounded with women all chatting animatedly with each other.

"Ladies! This is Mirabelle. I'll let you all introduce yourselves, and, sweetie, don't worry if you can't remember everyone's names. We're throwing a lot at you at once, and none of us expect you to remember it all in one day."

The only one I knew besides Donna was Elizabeth, and she jumped up from her seat to wrap me in a hug.

"I'm so glad you're back safe with us! I swear, we're not letting you out of our sight ever again."

Tears flowed down my cheeks as I held on to her. This woman was the reason I was here.

"Thank you, Elizabeth. Without you, I'd still be back there. You saved me."

She gave me another squeeze before shifting back to look me in the eye as she held my hands.

"Call me Bess. My dad is the only one who refuses to use my nickname now. And I'm glad I could help get you free—and Tabitha and Todd. I just wish I'd taken a closer look sooner. I should have dug deeper when your parents' estate was being processed. It wasn't right."

I gave her hands a squeeze before I pulled free. "You dug deeper when you could and I'm grateful. And a lawyer came to visit me a few times in Houston, she's confident she'll be able to get all my parents' assets back to me. Eventually. But honestly, I'm just grateful to have my life back."

Bess' eyes glossed over with tears, but she blinked them back.

"Okay, enough mushy stuff! Come and meet everyone,

then later we're going to take you out. Cindy's roller derby team is playing tonight and we're all going to go watch her kick ass."

I had no idea what roller derby was, or who Cindy was, but I loved that these ladies were already including me as though I was one of their own. I'd never had close girlfriends but had always wanted them. I couldn't believe it looked like I might have found a group that would accept me, issues and all.

Epilogue

Six weeks later
Donna

"Feels strange not being on the back of his bike, doesn't it?"

I smiled over at Zara as I set down the bowl of salad I'd just brought out. The club was on a poker run and she was right, normally I'd be on the back of Keys' bike, but today I was sitting out so Mirabelle could have the experience.

"Yeah, but I've had decades of enjoying the thrill of it. I'm more than happy to sit this one out so Mirabelle can go have some fun."

There were a number of old ladies here at the clubhouse helping to set up the barbecue lunch and chasing all the kids. The club had been having a baby boom for a few years now and it was showing. Toddlers running around, babies cooing or crying, and even a couple of old ladies about to add to the growing next generation of Charons.

"She seems to have settled in well. She's fit right in at Marie's."

I nodded as I followed Zara back to the kitchen. "She has. Especially now we're in the new place and she has her own bathroom. She's come so far. Cindy's been teaching her how to roller skate. Y'all taking her to that match of hers apparently sparked an interest. She's always happy when she comes home from working at Marie's. I'm glad she's fitting in so well. She's also been spending a lot of time at the gym."

Zara nodded. "She's Mac's star pupil in the self-defense classes. She wants to be strong and independent, which is great."

I nodded. "I know she mentioned to me after we'd first rescued her that she wanted to get into counseling, but I'm not sure she'll get through the course work with her memory issues. I think she's realizing that too. She's mentioned a few times this past week about becoming a personal trainer."

Zara grinned. "That would be great. We need a female instructor in there. Mac hasn't been able to find one. And helping people get strong and healthy will fulfill her desire to help others. I think it's a great idea. I'll mention it to Mac so he can look into courses so she can become certified. The memory thing is something we can work around. It doesn't have to prevent her from living a fulfilling life."

Considering Zara managed to live a full life even though she had narcolepsy and cataplexy, I didn't doubt she'd help Mirabelle learn how to cope with her own mental issues. As I'd known it would, the club had rallied around Maribelle to give her everything she needed to thrive.

"Getting her out of that facility was definitely the right move for her. I'm seriously wondering about whether we shouldn't move Tabitha out too, but Keys told me she'd refused to leave so long as her brother was there. And it's definitely the right place for him."

Zara sighed heavily. "That poor boy. So young to have had his world so horrifically torn apart. It's a fantastic facility, and if he's got the willpower to fight, they can help him do that. Just look at Sparrow. To see her now, you'd never guess what she's been through. Hopefully Tabitha can overcome her guilt. I know she still blames herself for Godfrey ever getting his hands on Todd."

Last year Mac and Zara had adopted Sparrow, a teen the club had rescued from a mob-run stable in L.A. She'd been sold into sexual slavery by her own mother to pay her drug debt. But the girl didn't have any quit in her and had made good use of her second chance with Mac and Zara. Their toddler, Cleo, loved her new big sister, and Sparrow clearly thought the little girl hung the moon. Sparrow was on the back of Mac's bike today and Cleo had thrown a fit when she'd seen her big sister ride off with her daddy.

"Where is Cleo? I can't hear her screaming anymore."

Zara rolled her eyes. "Lord save us from that one's temper. She wore herself out crying until she fell asleep. Hopefully she'll stay that way until they get back. She's gonna be hell until she's old enough to go out with Mac, and then we'll have to set up a schedule or something, so they get equal time on Mac's bike." She frowned. "Maybe I should put my own name on the damn thing so I get a turn too…"

Silk laughed and hip checked Zara as she walked past holding her son, Raven's hand.

"Don't you worry, Zara. Sparrow will be riding her own bike in a few years, same with Mirabelle."

Zara groaned. "Don't say that! I worry enough as it is."

Silk chuckled. "Well, don't think too much about what Cleo will do when she's a teenager then."

"The thought is enough to send me grey."

The rumble of Harleys filling the air ended our conversation as we all made our way through the clubhouse to watch them come in through the front gate.

Keys

Besides Em, I'd never had anyone other than Donna on the back of my bike. Until today. When we'd first taken off for the poker run earlier, it had hit me that it wasn't Em, that it would never be her again, but those thoughts were soon pushed aside when I looked in my mirror and saw Mirabelle's face. The wide grin as she closed her eyes and put her face in the wind.

This woman might be nearly thirty years old, but she was young at heart. Even with all the shit Godfrey had put her through, she still shone. Just like Donna,

Mirabelle had an inner light that could light up the whole world. It had been dimmed when she'd first come to live with us, but over the past six weeks, she'd grown stronger and more sure of herself, and now that light was shining brightly for all to see. And I wasn't the only one to notice.

We were now back at the clubhouse, enjoying the lunch the women had put together for us while we'd been riding, and I could see a couple bastards watching my girl.

"You gonna deal with that?"

There was some humor laced though Scout's voice, but I wasn't feeling it.

"Just you wait another ten years and it'll be Ariel that has men drooling over her. We'll see how fucking funny you think this shit is then."

Scout laughed. "That girl can already hold her own. I worry for the men she sets her sights on, not the other way around."

"I'm hoping Mirabelle's cut will keep any of the fuckers from actually approaching her."

As soon as possible, I'd gotten Mirabelle a cut with a daughter of the club patch. That patch screamed that if you wanted to even touch the one wearing it, you'd better be thinking forever and not a one-night stand.

"That'll keep our boys off her, but I'm not so sure about the Cowboys. Want me to have a quiet word with them?"

The Satan's Cowboys MC was a big club up north whose umbrella we technically came under. Several of their crew had come down to join in the poker run and at least two of them were eyeing Mirabelle in a way I didn't appreciate.

"I already had a word with Maverick. He said he'd tell his men her history and that she was protected."

Scout nodded. "I'll still keep my eye on them."

"Who we keeping an eye on?"

Mac strolled over with a couple of bottles of beer that he handed to us both before he took a swig of his own.

"The men eyeing my girl."

Mac turned to take in who we were talking about. "Oh, yeah. If they keep that shit up they're gonna get their asses beat."

"Damn straight."

Mac chuckled, "Not by you, old man. Have you seriously not noticed?"

I glared his way. "Not noticed what?"

Scout was smirking and trying not to laugh, so clearly he knew.

With a growl, I switched my glare from Mac to Scout. "One of you better tell me whose ass I'm gonna have to beat."

"Nah, man. It's way more fun this way. I can't believe you haven't seen it. Guess he's been careful when you're around."

I narrowed my eyes at Scout, the club president. A man whom I thought was my friend.

"Just you wait. One day it'll be Ariel who has a secret admirer and I won't tell you shit."

He smirked at me again. "I'll just make sure I teach her

how to shoot. That way, she can take care of it herself."

Mac laughed. "Don't let him fool you. He'll be squirming as bad as you are now. Ah, fuck. Dammit."

He turned and strode across the yard and I spun to see what had set him off. When I saw Sparrow sneaking closer to where Jazz was standing with a couple of other brothers, I forgot all about Mirabelle and her apparent harem of admirers and got ready to watch Mac go papa bear on either Sparrow's or Jazz's ass.

"He won't touch her. I think everyone in the club has pulled that boy aside to warn him she's too young."

"Don't look like he's the one doing the chasing, brother. That girl's got a crush going on."

Scout nodded. "That, she does. Good to see her behavin' like a normal teen. And that's why I ain't telling you who's watching Mirabelle. He knows the rules. She's a daughter of the club. If he steps up publicly to make a claim on her, we'll know he's serious. Until then, he's just letting her be a normal fucking teenager. And much like Sparrow, your girl needs to be free to do what young, single women do, brother. No matter how much you want her not to."

I frowned as I took another swig of my beer. "It's not that I don't want her to, it's that I don't want her getting hurt."

"Pain is part of life, my friend. None of us are immune, and we all fall at some point. But like you and me, she now has this whole club at her back to kick her ass if she forgets to get the fuck back up when she does."

Heat flashed through me at his words and I took another swig of beer to give me a minute.

"Thanks for that. What you and Mac did that day? Probably not only saved my marriage, but my life."

Scout clapped me on the shoulder. "Just sorry it took us so long to see how bad you were struggling, brother. Should have kicked your ass years ago."

"Better late than never, Prez."

"Indeed."

Silence fell between us as we watched Mac drag his adopted daughter away from Jazz and back over to the other single women. I couldn't help but think Mac had better get used to that because Cleo was gonna be a hell-raiser when she was older. But we'd all help keep her in line and safe, because that's what the Charon MC was all about. Protecting our family.

I'd never been happier, or prouder, of the patch I wore than I was today.

The End

Other Charon MC Books:

Book 1:
Inking Eagle

Eagle & Silk

Book 2:
Fighting Mac

Mac & Zara

Book 3:
Chasing Taz

Taz & Zara

Book 4:
Claiming Tiny

Tiny & Mercedes (Missy)

Book 5:
Saving Scout

Scout & Marie

Book 6:
Tripping Nitro

Nitro & Cindy

Book 7:
Scout's Legacy

Scout & Marie

Book 8:

Mac's Destiny

Mac & Zara

Book 9:

Losing Bash

Bash

Book 10:

Finding Needles

Needles & Bess

Book 11:

Forging Blade

Blade & Veronica